SEDONA UPSET

ANASTASIA ALEXANDER

The Sedona Upset

Published by Elegant Elephant Books, Inc

Printed in the United States of America

ISBN: 978-1948410090

Year of first printing 2020

CHAPTER 1

Maggie

I BLINKED into the harsh sunlight at my new home just outside Tucson: adobe… flat… with saguaro outlining the place and, instead of lush green grass in the yard, a bed of jagged red rock. This was nothing like LA. My home. It was my choice to move here. Tucson, adobe, and JT were my future. And heat, I thought as I stared through the windshield of the truck. Lots and lots of heat.

Sweat dotted my brow, the back of my neck, and stuck to the rest of my body like a used lollypop. The piercing 118-degrees wrapped me with a suffocating grip as the news announced on the radio the day was "too hot to fly."

One hundred and eighteen degrees. Could humans survive that? I glanced over at JT, my fiancé, and clenched my fists. I could do it. If I could handle childbirth years ago, a gut-wrenching divorce a few years later, and been turned into the villain on a TV bachelor show viewed by millions of people, maybe tens of millions, what was heat? Hot, that was sure, but it was dry. That supposedly would make it better. That and being with the man I loved. The man who made me feel more myself than I ever felt in my life.

I gazed over the brown landscape as we pulled up to the house, my stomach twisted into knots. My fiancé, JT, the multimillionaire who lived here, and the famous bachelor on the TV show, was also a rough and tough cowboy. Well, not that rough or tough, but he did have a beard and a horse, which he rode after work.

At least that was what he told me. We didn't really know each other that well, but I was here to discover all the mysteries of this man who sent electricity through me, and the person I couldn't stop thinking about. I wanted to know everything about him. I wanted to know if he wore slippers in the house. Did he start the morning watching the sunrise? Did he toss his socks in a drawer or roll them tight and aligned?

"Excited, dear?" JT snapped off his seatbelt in the truck. He took my hand and gave it a soft squeeze, sending comfort up my forearm. "This is your new home. I hope you like it."

I flushed and whispered, "Thank you."

I never imagined, in all my thirty-odd years of life, I would land in east Tucson, Arizona, of all places. Not on the top of my list of places to visit, but I, Maggie Chambers, won JT Devonshire's heart after a fierce battle in the dating show, *Millionaire Engagement,* and another battle after the show. So here I was ready to begin my new life, even though I had no idea how I would fit into it or what it would look like.

I inhaled the fire-hot air and concluded I must love him to be here. So far, Tucson offered miles of brown land-scape, which JT suggested was multi-shades of green, and ground squirrels that darted across the roadway playing chicken with the motorists, and he braked for every one of them. Every single one.

The frequent braking behavior gave my belongings, which followed in the diesel truck and trailer, a good shakedown, but I guess it saved the little devils, which was what JT was focused on. I guess the fact he loved animals so much was endearing, but I couldn't help staring down the barrel of the reality of making this place my home with native bunnies and javelinas running by.

To be honest, I hadn't totally thought through leaving sunny, green Southern California for this final frontier of the Wild West, but JT was the guy I wanted to be with, and his life was here. With ground squirrels and heat.

Before JT and I got back together, but after he broke up with the show's winner, Milly, he had asked me, "Why did you just take off?"

I had opted for a Marriott instead of camping with other women when we were shooting the show. At the time, I'd replied with a quip, "Marriott's budget rooms are my favorite camping spot."

He shook his head with a sadness about him that somehow made me feel bad for my snap response.

"You don't like roughing it?" he asked like it was head-line news. Underneath, what he was really asking was, *Do you bail on everything you don't want to do?*

Which, when it came to roughing it in the outdoors, of course, I would bail. I wasn't built for the wilderness. I was a more of a high-maintenance lily who wilted when the weather wasn't between sixty and ninety degrees. That was why I had lived in California.

Maybe being a delicate lily would be too demanding for a person like JT. Being like that might suggest to him that I didn't belong in his world. If he ever thought that, he wouldn't keep me around. He sent me packing once because he didn't want to be with someone who couldn't stick with difficulty. I was going to show him I could stick it out. And this time, I wasn't going to bail. I tightened my fists. I could do it. I knew I could.

JT leaned over and kissed me gently. "Let's get out and introduce you to my world and see how you do."

So, it was a test?

He hopped out of the truck.

It was a test. Had to be. He wanted to know how I fit here with his big-money, low-maintenance home, with no mustangs in sight—car *or* horse. I have never been a southwestern country person. Never wanted to be. But I could do it.

What it lacked in oceans and mild temperatures it made up in... I climbed out of the truck, stepping onto gravel rocks. I wiggled my legs to release the travel ache and nerves that bubbled up, trying to find a redeeming element of this place.

I stepped toward the house, the rocks crunching under my feet, until sudden pain projected into my ankle. I yelped. Pain shot like someone had thrust several needles into my skin.

"Everything okay?" called JT from somewhere behind the trailer.

I looked down at my right foot. A thin green cactus with white fangs wedged into my ankle. I sucked in my breath as tears stung my eyes. I could do this. "Yes," I called out to put on a good face. The pain of the pricks had radiated through my body. The cactus was *eating* me.

I stared down at my foot. I wore three-hundred-dollar sandals with sparkly faux diamonds decorating their straps. Wrong shoes for this situation but, on a good note, my purple nail polish contrasted well with the light-tan dirt, greyish gravel, and the rhinestones. I could do this.

I stood balanced on my right foot and carefully angled my shoe, so the sole of my sandal brushed at the cactus. I kicked to knock it off my ankle.

"Ouch!" I cried out as the cactus wedged deeper into my skin. Drops of blood welled up. How was I going to get the thorns out of my flesh?

JT strolled around the trailer, decked in his cowboy hat and cowboy boots, looking like this was his terrain in the bright sunlight. "What's the matter?"

I turned toward him and peered down at my ankle, unshed tears prickling my eyes.

His eyes followed mine and he picked up his pace, talking low and calm. "That's a jumping cactus."

"Yes. And they're flesh-eating," I said.

He laughed as he put his hands on my hips and lifted me into his arms. "They're vicious. You have to watch out around here."

I folded my arm around his strong neck and held on.

I blinked to keep the involuntary tears from falling.

This was the height of being a helpless damsel if I couldn't even get out of a truck without getting hurt. I felt my cheeks flame with heat. This was exactly what not to do.

JT swooped me into his arms and carried me toward the garage of his house like I weighed no more than a bag of potatoes. The muscles in his arms and shoulders rippled as he moved. He had a musky scent I loved.

I rested my right hand on his shoulder as he shifted me in his arms. "It just jumped out and got me. I'm serious. It lunged at me."

He chuckled. "They're called jumping cactus for a reason. They're known to hook into any passing animals or humans. You can't live here without having several jumping cactus experiences." He glanced at my foot. "We might want to get you some better shoes."

I didn't want to become the cliché of the Southwest stomping around here in cowboy boots. That had to be hot and look horrible. "Like what?"

"Something with thick soles. I have had a few go right through my tennis shoes."

My stomach tightened.

"Cowboy boots work well."

Naturally. He set me down on my feet carefully in front of the metal screen side door. I peered through it to a very clean garage with orderly stacks of stuff. JT dug into his pocket, pulled out his keys to unlock the door, and went to pick me up again so I wouldn't have to hobble in.

I held out my palms, not wanting to appear completely helpless. "I can get it."

He nodded like that was reasonable and took off and found a stool, which he set in the center of the first parking stall. I hobbled over, and by the time I reached the stool he had returned with pliers.

I crossed my wounded ankle over my left knee as he tugged on the cactus. Once the green part of the cactus was gone, five white needles with a cross at the top remained pierced into my flesh.

"Sorry about this." I sucked in my breath and winced at the pain.

"It happens."

"Am I too high maintenance for you?"

He let go of my hands and looked me in the eyes. "You are high maintenance, Mags."

My heart skipped a beat. That wasn't good. Not good at all. "You think we're too different? Do you think I'm too city for Tucson?"

He looked around us. "This is a low maintenance world. Cactus and mustangs."

"So, I don't belong here?"

He smiled, like that was an antidote. My heart slowed. "You're going to light the place up."

"The mustangs will like that." Not at all sure if that would work, since I didn't know any mustangs. They were horses, weren't they? Or maybe they were cars? I'd have to google.

With steady hands and swift confidence, JT plucked out the needles as I clenched my teeth. My heartbeat picked up.

"This hurts."

He nodded. "It does."

"I love how you just drop everything and take care of me."

He patted my forearm. "It's my job."

7

It was sexy how he just took care of the situation. Me. No fuss. Just did what needed to be done.

After the last needle was out, he stepped back. "There. Let's get some Neosporin on it and a Band-Aid. You'll be as good as new."

The sting of the punctures had heightened my senses. The burn simmered in my ankle as JT rambled around to find the first aid supplies. Moments later, he was back by my side patching up my wounds with a soft touch. He even took my ankle to his lips and kissed it right next to my wounds, sending shivers up my leg.

"All better," he said with a teasing smile playing on his lips.

I laughed. "All better." I stood and extended my arms for a hug.

He folded me into his strong embrace, pressing me into him like he wanted to hold onto me and would never let me go. My pulse increased. I liked how desired I felt with his small actions.

"You never held any of the other girls on the show they way you hold me."

"That's because I didn't love them."

Feeling my heart swell with the luxury of being with a man who wanted to be with me, and was willing to step up and take care of me when I suffered a cactus attack, I squeezed him tight, surprised to discover just how solid he was. "Thank you, Doctor Dreamy."

He shook his head. "I'm not a doctor. I just play one in my garage."

I laughed and ran the back of my hand down his chest,

ready to move in for another embrace, but he said, "All good? Should we go unload?"

I let my hand slide away. JT was the CEO of a cell-tower company, always wheeling and dealing and making millions. I'd have to get used to his goal-focused way.

"Sure," I said brightly. "Let's get back into the heat, yeah?"

He laughed and was already walking out of the garage.

Mission man.

Within a few seconds, he had opened the back of the trailer as I hobbled back over to the passenger seat to fix my lipstick. A squirrel darted by me disappearing in a hole in the dirt, alerting me that across the street strolled a thin coyote, tail high in the air, scavenging the neighborhood.

I froze and stopped myself from screaming. JT didn't scream at wildlife, so I wouldn't either. The poor, scrawny animal lumbered diagonally across a distant neighbor's yard. My heart shook fiercely as I waited to make sure he was going to keep going wherever he was headed.

"Coyote," I called out.

"Cool." JT's voice came out muffled.

"Yeah," I muttered.

A series of banging sounds came from behind the trailer. "Maggie, could I get a hand?" JT called.

Glancing to keep track of the coyote's progress, I turned my focus to prepare myself to find which of my belongings had been shattered or destroyed. Who knew what had happened during the eight-hour trip, moving me from the land of city lights and opportunity to this desert of only weather-beaten earth. And squirrels. No mustangs, yet.

I slid my sunglasses down off the top of my head as the fierce sun pressed. I hobbled to JT to see how I could help, still surprised at how the heated air made it hard to breathe. Maybe seeing a coyote strolling the neighborhood also added to my inability to find air. Or, the heat I wasn't used to.

JT stood on the trailer bed holding up the door, muscles popping under his shirt. I cleared my throat. He held a steel gadget in his hand, about three inches long. Uh oh. Did he want me to do something with that? I dashed another look in the coyote's direction. The predator was nowhere in sight. "Yes, baby?"

He was bent at the waist, his wide hands gripping the strange gadget. "Would you mind holding this for me so I can lock the lever?"

Sounded simple enough. I scurried around him to the tailgate. I put my hand on the metal for leverage to hoist me up next to him. The moment my hand touched the metal, the heat singed my skin.

I yelped, shaking my hand, and JT's eyes swiveled to me. I smiled again, brighter than ever.

"What happened?"

I closed my eyes. "I burnt myself on the metal."

He dropped the hitch. It clanged as it fell. "Seriously?" He stumbled over boxes to reach me. "Let me see it." He held out his hand.

I flushed. "It's just a little burn."

He held my fingers up in the air to examine them. "You need to ice them?"

I shook my head. "I'm all good." I hoped my voice sounded chipper and not in pain.

A corner of his mouth curled up. "A kiss better?"

"Sure." I smiled brightly.

He gently pulled my hand to his lips and kissed ever so lightly right below the burn. A cluster of excitement shot through me. He was being sweet again.

"Anything else you need me to kiss?" He gave me a slow-building smile.

Heat rushed through me. "My cheek." I tipped my cheek up to him.

"That is a sign that you're all better." He gave a slow kiss on my cheek sending more chills through me.

"Thank you." I climbed back onto the trailer, but it was a struggle.

JT hurried behind me and hefted me up by pushing my backside. I yelped in surprise. "What is it you want me to help you with?"

He jumped into the trailer as though it wasn't a feat and passed by me, giving my forearm a squeeze of affection, and reached farther into the trailer to fiddle with a chain. His musky cologne kept swarming at my senses, distracting me, and making my heart pound.

I fiddled with a box and pulled out a loose rag to use between the steel and my fingers in case the metal was just as hot inside the trailer. I put my hand next to his to hold the lever. Heat flushed my face, but not only because he was hot as sin. Our heads leaned in close as he fiddled with something above us. Leaning over on my tippy-toes, I kissed his neck. He straightened with a jerk, and barely missed hitting his head on the truck.

"Whoa!"

"Sorry, you were so irresistible with those muscles

flexing and smelling so manly. Ooh la la." I waggled my eyebrows up and down.

He reddened.

I laughed. "I'm embarrassing you."

"So?" he said, straight-faced with an air of intensity. There was something almost charming in the fact he was trying to play it matter-of-fact.

"The Great JT blushes."

"Don't tell anyone," he grumbled.

I slapped my hand to my chest. "I'll do my best to resist your incredible sexiness until a more appropriate time and keep your response my secret." I peered up at him coyly.

He rolled his eyes. "Keep holding that," he said, all business, but he did pat my arm reassuringly.

I could tell how he had become president of his company. That was super attractive and scary at the same time. I hoped he would never turn that CEO nature on me. My eyes flickered over my disheveled belongings. Boxes had slipped and fallen, and my dining table limped to the left with a broken leg. I closed my eyes. I'd owned that table for more than fifteen years. It overflowed with memories of Jackson, my former husband, and the period of my life when I raised my son.

That table was where I'd served seventeen birthday dinners for Austin. Where I sat on Saturday mornings to write checks and pay our bills. The table where I made dinners for my husband and son thinking we were building a permanent family.

I opened my eyes and peered into the dim shadows of the trailer... of my past.

Time to let it go. Time to let everything of my past marriage go. Time to move into my future with JT.

At my side, I heard JT mutter a low curse. "Oh, no." He pushed his hat back on his head and scratched his forehead. "I'm so sorry. It must have been the—"

Ground squirrel.

"The hill. I'm sorry." He moved into the trailer, pushing boxes out of his way. "I'll get it fixed. I know a guy—"

"It's okay," I said loudly, cutting him off. "It's just…" I swallowed. "It's just a table." My shoulders lowered, accepting the fate of my furniture.

Besides the table, I had brought my big armoire. It was a stunning piece of furniture, but I had no idea how we would get it off this moving van or where to put in JT's house. In California, I had asked the film crew to help and kind of forgot to tell JT.

"Um, baby," I called out as he dug deep into the moving van. I picked up the lightest box I could find, thinking maybe I could climb out of the trailer with it without getting hurt. "Do you think the neighbors would help us haul the furniture in?"

"Nope."

I stopped in my tracks and saw part of his arm behind boxes. "Why not? That's what neighbors do."

"Don't worry about it," he called out from between the boxes. "I will handle it."

I put the box down and crawled over the other boxes to see his eyes. "Do you always handle everything?"

"Yes."

"Why?"

He looked over at me. "When my mom was dying, I

promised her I would take care of Dad and everything else." He shrugged. "I got used to it."

That was, in a sense, sweet and upsetting.

JT fiddled with boxes and cleared a path, shifting from his story. "How are we going to move the furniture? It's heavy."

With large ruffling sounds from the back of the truck. "I'll do it," he said, winded.

"How?"

He shrugged. "I'll figure it out."

"We could call the Mormon missionaries. They're always hunting for service projects."

"It's easier to just do it ourselves."

That wasn't true. "People like to help."

He wiped his sweaty forehead, and peered one eye down at me. "Other people get in the way."

That was certainly one way of looking at it. JT was being much more of a loner than I thought of him being. "Well, yes, while they're carrying armoires from moving vans," I clarified. "That's exactly when we *want* people in our way."

He turned from the back of the van, a huge, wide, and extremely heavy box cradled in his arms. "I don't need help."

I lifted my brows. "Ever?"

He shifted the box, his gaze pinned on mine. "Rarely."

That extremely wide, extremely heavy box slipped in his arms an inch, tipping to the side. The contents rumbled inside. JT's forearm muscles twitched.

I lifted my brows higher.

He shifted the box level again and lifted his brows even higher.

So. An eyebrow war.

We stood there, eyebrows up, the heavy box pressing into his forearm and sweat dripping down my back.

"Want me to help with that?" I asked sweetly, not holding back a gentle teasing smile.

"I'm fine." His voice was a little strained. "Don't worry about it. I don't want you to get hurt anymore today. Okay?"

He was trying to redirect my focus. "How long?" I asked.

"How long until what?"

"Until you ask for help?"

He grinned. "Never. How long 'til you get out of my way?"

I crossed my arms. "When you ask nicely."

"Please get out of my way," he said nicely. He kissed the side of my head as he bustled by, not needing help at all.

Curse him. The things you learn about a person when moving.

It didn't take him long to return. "I have something you can help with if you are up for it?"

I scooted up to him and pecked him on the cheek. "Okay."

A smile crept onto his face as I hurried to the back of the truck.

"Hold on," he called out. "Give me a second to secure the door and a ramp. Don't want you to burn yourself again."

I sucked in my breath. I couldn't help but like that he

wanted to take care of me and was worried I would get burnt. My hand still hurt, and a nasty blister had already popped out in a white bubble, not to mention that my lower back ached from jumping up on the bumper, and my ankle felt like more needles had pressed into it.

As I waited I, I lifted up my ankle and saw two more thin clear needles. I yanked at them, then ran my hand along my chewed-up ankle to see if any more of those sneaky needles had implanted in my skin. I couldn't find any.

JT returned with a dolly and straps, maneuvering around me. I flushed and picked up the same light box again to follow him to the house, not wanting to appear useless or like a klutz.

"Baby, it shouldn't take us long to unload this stuff. Maybe we could swim to cool down after this?"

His eyes flickered to me briefly. "Maybe."

Not encouraging. I decided not to question him on that answer. That would be high maintenance, and I would act chill as a cucumber slice in a glass of cold water.

He must have seen the disappointment in my face, because he added, "Let's see if we have time before dark. It cools down a lot in the evenings."

"Hot tub?" I batted my eyes.

"Don't have one."

"Oh," my voice came out with more disappointment than intended. I had just assumed that because he lived in a mansion with a pool, a hot tub would be an automatic side accessory. Apparently, even though he had money, he leaned more toward a simple lifestyle.

"Disappointed?"

I shrugged, trying to not make a big deal about it. "It's fine."

"You're a hot tub fan?"

I shrugged again, bigger this time. I didn't want to come across as demanding and needy. "I like a good soak every now and then. With a place like this, I bet it would be lovely to come out in the blackness of the evening and sit in a tub with a glass of wine and let the hot water ease out all the aches and pains."

He strolled ahead of me. "That's an excellent idea."

I brightened, then quickly shifted the box in my arms, which felt heavier and heavier as I followed him toward the open garage.

"The nights can be stunning," he said over his shoulder. "We can do that sometime if you want."

"Yes, I want."

He glanced back. Our gazes caught. "I'll take care of everything."

That made me happy. But the vague note of grimness in his tone made me uneasy.

"I'll be fine without—"

"If you want it, we'll get it."

And that was that.

I wasn't going to fight to deny myself a hot tub. "I'd love that!"

The box I was carrying started to slip out of my grasp. I stumbled into a bush, which scratched my calf on the opposite side from the cactus bite.

I stopped to heft the load up on a bent leg and secure it higher in my arms, wincing from the pain. Sweat had already coated me like I had taken a shower.

A flicker caught my attention.

There, on my right, in between the rocks and under the bush, a multi-colored snake unfolded itself out of a tight ball.

His black, brown, and orange colors flashed in the sunlight.

I struggled to squeeze air into my lungs.

He moved. The reptile uncurled and started to slither. A high-pitched wheezing slipped through my lips.

I couldn't take my eyes off him as he rippled away, gliding over the rocks. At my strangled sound, JT dropped his box at the garage entrance and sprinted back.

"What!" he shouted.

I stared at him, my mouth open, the box in my arms about to fall. "S—s—snake!"

He grabbed a shovel out of the garage and was on the move. I watched as he leaned down, pulled his jeans tight against his hard thighs, and... picked the thing up on the shovel.

"What are you doing?" I whisper-asked.

He carefully lifted the twisting creature and, with measured steps, strolled past me.

I stumbled back a few steps. "I don't want to meet him," I almost shrieked.

He gave a little laugh as the snake coiled and turned on the shovel head. "I'm putting him back in the wild." He lifted the shovel high and dumped the creature on the other side of the fence, then turned. He planted the shovel tip in the ground, hooked an arm over the handle, and grinned at me, looking every inch the cowboy.

"What if that snake bit you..."

He pressed his lips together to hold back a grin. "You'll be fine."

Apparently, my reaction was a sit-com for him. I wanted to say more, but remembered Low Maintenance Maggie. I pressed my lips together, and he kissed the top of my forehead.

Score one for low maintenance.

"I thought you were going to kill him," I said, somewhat accusatorially.

JT shook his head against that idea. "I returned him to his home. He has more right to be here than we do."

"Are there others out there?" I nodded to the wilds beyond his fence.

"Yup. Lots. You'll get used to it."

I shook my head. "No, I won't."

He laughed and strode over, shovel in hand. "I'll teach you everything you need to know about watching out for all the deadly critters."

"And deadly cactus," I added.

He dropped the shovel and slid his arms under the box in my arms, taking it from me.

"What if I don't want to learn?" I muttered as I followed him into the shady garage, where it was about ten degrees cooler.

"You don't want to die, do you?"

"Are those my only options?

He set the box down and looked at me for a long minute. Sweat trickled down the back of my neck as I avoided his eyes.

"Come here," he said softly.

I shuffled toward him.

"Closer."

I came within a step of him, his hard body so near I could smell his musk scent again. He hooked a hand around the back of my neck and tugged me to him. He bent and pressed a kiss to the top of my head. "You're in Arizona now, Mags. This is your home. There are snakes and cactus and bobcats and coyotes, and skies that never end and sunsets that last for hours and air so clean you can breathe."

An uneasiness moved through me. His mouth was soft on my head, his breath warm through my hair.

"And there's you," I whispered.

He pressed another kiss to my head. "You and me, I'll take care of everything," he promised.

"That's what you do," I whispered.

I felt him nod. "That's what I do. Come on, I want to show you the house. You need a break from the outside. Let's give you a tour of where you'll be staying before we finish unloading."

He flopped his long arm around my shoulder and guided me toward the front gate. Getting inside sounded like I great idea, but I pivoted toward the truck.

"But my stuff… don't we need to close the door or something?" All I owned in the world was in the trailer. All of it.

He laughed. "This isn't LA. Your stuff will be fine."

I peered at the truck one more time, not sure if I trusted his word. My heart fluttered. Thieves lurked in all points of the world, not just LA. An open trailer with packed boxes was an inviting invitation to come steal. I had googled Tucson's safety statistics before coming. It didn't rate high on the scorecard for safety. It was never good to gamble with fate.

JT must have seen my worry. "Hardly anybody comes out to the east side. It's too far a drive from the main part of town."

I squished my lips together. I didn't blame the thieves for not taking the drive here—at least forty-five minutes from the freeway, and the entire drive was Pot Hole City. Hard on the suspension, plus the scenery consisted of mostly rundown stores, cactus, and brown dirt.

Granted, JT had neighbors several acres away on either side of his house, but those houses were adobe and blended into the wilderness as much as the wildlife and plants. Horses and cows had waved their tails as we drove in, but I'd seen no exercisers hitting the streets.

No lingering neighbors gathered around the mailboxes to discuss the heat and, as of yet, no neighbor labored on their lawns, building their connection with nature. No children made noise, no neighborhood sounds reached my ears, except the occasional grind of a distant drill of a construction worker and the tweeting of a bird.

This would not be a place I would see any Jehovah's Witnesses traveling in packs to save the world. And, once we had passed the city limits, I didn't see Mormon missionaries with their dark suits, white shirts, and nametags. It was too hot and too far, even for God.

"I'll close it if it makes you feel better," JT said.

"Thanks, baby."

Watching him stroll to the trailer in his cowboy boots and hat, I had a sudden chill. I had truly moved to the boonies. What could I possibly do here to have a life?

CHAPTER 2

T

MAGGIE LOOKED stunning standing in the sunlight, surveying me returning from the truck with lips pressed together as though holding back her words, her truth. Bags lurked under her eyes. She seemed frazzled, with worn-out makeup and beads of sweat outlining her flattened hair. It had been a lot for her to leave the beach, her job, and her best friend to move to Tucson. I hoped she could find her place here and it would be worth it for her to be with me and closer to her son.

She'd taken the jumping cactus in her ankle like a trouper, but when she spotted the napping snake, her lips had quivered. She was scared of animals. It was a bit charming, actually, that she found this world so different. I hoped as she spent more time here, she'd learn that being closer to wildlife was good for the soul. My biggest job was to ensure the smoothest ride possible for her, be her shock absorber until she learned to appreciate Old Pueblo.

I wrapped my arm around her shoulder, pulling her closer to me. "Let's get you indoors."

She laughed as she followed my lead through the nine-foot wrought-iron gate and into the front of the house. The outdoor sitting area was sheltered from the sun with a partially open roof overhead and rust-orange wooden-paneled walls.

Maggie hurried over to the couch, sat, and plopped her arms out against the armrest for a couple of moments, taking in the scene like she was the new owner. A ripple of nerves chased through me. It was strange having someone new in my home.

She scooted back on the cushion, her feet coming off the ground and dangling in the air like a little girl sitting in a grown-up chair. "Have you ever noticed most furniture is meant for big people? It's complete discrimination."

Maggie could be really funny sometimes. "Can't say I have."

That had been Irene's favorite spot in the house. She'd sat there as twilight turned into night, doing puzzles, talking to friends on the phone, not talking to me at all. Of course, I didn't talk to her much either. We had nothing to say. We'd sat three feet apart for twenty years and never just… chatted.

Maggie coughed, breaking my unpleasant reverie. I jerked my gaze to hers and stared for a second, then burst out laughing. "Short person discrimination, huh?" I moved toward her.

"I'm almost never able to have my feet touch the ground and sit all the way back," she continued. "How am I supposed to look dignified with my legs dangling in the air? No one is going to take me serious like that."

People took Irene seriously. Always. She wasn't one for fun.

"The only time they make small chairs is on airplanes," Maggie continued in her happy chattering bubble. "That's ridiculous because often I'm squished, and I'm short." She sank deeper into the couch as she spoke, and didn't pause to hear my response. "I could see drinking iced tea out here in the early afternoons together."

Irene had binoculars, a bird book, and a notebook in which she wrote with precise handwriting as if the record was crucial. She jotted down the birds she spotted: hummingbird, wren, and woodpecker.

"Do you want tea?"

Maggie's question brought my attention back to her. Tea. She wanted tea. "If tea on a porch will make you happy, tea on the porch you'll have. Pick up iced tea next time you're at the grocery store."

Just keep talking to me. The unbidden thought flashed through my mind and scared the hell out of me. It reeked of desperation. Of need. I loved Maggie, but I didn't need her. If I did, I'd be weak, and my job was to take care of business. I'd been doing it since I was fifteen years old and my mom died, and my dad turned into a workaholic. Taking care of business and people was all I knew.

Her mouth opened slightly at my suggestion. "I'll be doing the grocery shopping?"

"I'll get you set up with a checking account to take care of household expenses."

Maggie sank deeper onto the couch, eyeing the sun-bleached, high sky, and the brown scrub brush. It seemed like she was surreptitiously scanning for the snake.

"You'll learn to love it here, maybe even the snakes."

She flickered a glance up to me, full of doubt. "I don't remember this furniture when we were shooting for the show."

"We cleared it out so the producers could create a fantasy environment for the TV audience."

She nodded like that made sense, her nose pinching in the way that made her beautiful. "Was your wife short?"

We had never talked about my wife. Maggie had never asked about her. I knew it would come sooner or later. We couldn't really know each other if we didn't know each other's romantic past. It was like the debit column in a ledger—it had to be dealt with.

I shoved my hands into my pocket and forced myself to lower my gaze to Maggie's. Her tone was casual, light, no hint of feeling threatened. "Yes, my dear, she was short."

I worked to keep my tone as light and as casual as hers. It would be nice if we could talk about Irene when we needed to, which shouldn't be often. "Even shorter than you, but you are a lot different from her."

Maggie perked up in her seat. "How's that?"

I leaned back. I pushed my cowboy hat up. "Well, let's see… Irene was shorter and more serious."

Her eyes locked onto mine. "You don't think I am serious?"

I smiled, amused. "No, Mags. You're a breath of fresh

air. Fun. You lighten up my day. That is one of the things I love about you."

Her thin lips pressed together. "But you married something a lot different than that before. How does that work?"

I shrugged. "A different stage of my life. You're exactly what I need now."

Bright. Effervescent. Fully engaged. High maintenance maybe, but easy-going. High heels and hot tubs were no problem. I could meet those needs easily.

Maggie leaned back farther on the couch. "I'm glad." She squinted from the sun in her eyes, but I could tell she liked what I said. "I'd love to sit out here with you and take in the sunset. That would be so romantic."

I chuckled. My dear had no sense of direction in this place. I extended my hand out to help her to her feet. "The house faces south. You won't be able to see the sunset from this spot."

She climbed to her feet. "Oh no."

I put out my hand on her forearm and the gentle sway of her back to steady her. "We'd have to go into the backyard, but we don't have much of a view from there. We could go hiking up Mount Lemmon to see it. It's stunning. You can look over the whole valley. You like hiking?"

She took a moment to turn back and look at me. "I'll walk a long way for a romantic picnic with you... and Greek olives."

"Greek olives, hun?"

She nodded, batting her eyelashes. "I love them."

"Greek olives it is then."

She rubbed her tummy.

I smiled and swung open the wooden front door and followed her in, feeling deeply satisfied. She was perfectly ready to take a hike with me even though hikes weren't her speed. I'd make sure she got Greek olives. A match made in heaven.

Cool air-conditioned air greeted us as we stepped inside the house. She circled around in silence, her gaze skipping over everything. Of course, she had seen parts of my place before on the show, but the show had staged my place with their own furniture. This was the first time for her to see it as I really lived.

Her gaze lingered on my favorite tan leather couch. The place I loved to sit after an especially grueling day. I'd had the thing since before I married Irene and, over her objections, I'd put it smack in the center of our living room. It was well-worn, a bit ragged along the seams, but it was the most comfortable thing I owned, and I loved it. Irene never liked the couch. Maybe Mags would see it differently… although her feet would dangle off that more than any other furniture in the house.

A ridge of tension rode along my spine as I waited, giving her time to check it out. She continued to stare at it. A tiny frown edged at the corner of her lips. "Looks… comfy."

"It's a bit worn, and color is a bit off," I offered, making it okay if she didn't like it.

Maggie shook her head. "Looks like you really like it."

"I do." I was relieved I wouldn't have to fight with her about it.

"Let's see the rest of the house."

I led her to my bedroom, freshly touched up by the

cleaning lady. It smelled of lemon freshener. I stopped in front of the bed and she stopped by my side. "This is where I sleep." I reached out and stroked her silky hair. My bed was made with military corners. A vitamin C bottle sat on the nightstand, along with a stack of business books.

Maggie took her time. Her eyes moved first to the bed, then to the empty tan walls. I had taken down all the paintings. Only the rugged nail holes remained.

Once upon a time, a series of Thomas Kinkade cottage paintings had hung there. Irene hammered the nails and put them up when we first got married, and they'd mocked me with their idyllic lies those first nights after she passed, until I ripped them down.

On the night before Irene's funeral, I took all three of the paintings off the wall and marched them outside, past the horse corral, into the scrub brush. In the middle of the night, I'd raked out a huge bare spot and tossed the Kinkades in a pile. I'd gathered loose wood and built a huge bonfire of branches until the flames lapped high above my head and smoke filled the air.

My skin had tingled with heat as I tossed the paintings into the flames. The fire roared up and the paint bubbled until colored tears ran across the wilting canvases. Flames consumed the paintings as I burned the lies they told me about what would never be.

My brother-in-law and business partner Dimitri flipped his lid about the cost of what I'd burned in the fire, but I didn't care. Dimitri was the only person I'd ever talked to about my grieving, yet I hadn't said much to him.

What was there to say?

"No paintings?" Maggie asked with a sideways glance,

bringing me back to the present. "You against them?"

I looked at Maggie and her sexy blue eyes. I wanted to tell her I couldn't handle things on the wall reminding me of what could have been.

Maggie cleared her throat waiting for me to answer. To tell her about my blank walls and broken dreams.

I opened my mouth and nothing came out. I lifted my shoulders in a shrug. "Yeah, no paintings."

Maggie clapped her hands together. "We should put our wedding pictures up here."

My throat constricted.

"There's enough room to blow up the wedding pictures big."

Women had a way of taking over a place if a man wasn't careful. To change the subject, I asked, "Did you realize this is one of the first times we've had a chance to be together without the prying eye of the camera?"

Maggie smiled. "That's true. This is our second chance. Maybe I won't mess it up."

I brushed her hair onto her back, revealing her slender neck. "Maybe this time *we* won't mess it up."

Her face lit up from that. She wandered into the master bathroom. "No bathtub in the master suite?"

It looked like she was well on her way to taking over my place. With her energy, she'd have this place changed in no time. "There's one down the hall with the guest bedrooms."

I wasn't going to explain I had the bathroom completely redone to make it easier for Irene to shower. Climbing in and out of a tub had gotten too rough. A shower chair and showerhead were more manageable until, at the end, when the nurses sponge-bathed her. I closed my eyes to rid my mind of Irene's grey face, her thin body. The cancer had consumed her.

I had put all my grief in a box. In honor of my wife, I'd open that box on her birthday once a year. No. Other. Day. Not today. Not tomorrow. Not now.

Maggie caressed my hand. "Baby, you okay?"

I squeezed her fingers, mentally closing the box before showing her the rest of the house.

By the time we made it to the greenhouse where I grew Irene's flowers, Maggie noticed scratches on the cement. "The film crew must have been really hard on this place."

"That they were."

"They were hard on a lot of things," she muttered.

The media had not been nice to Maggie or Milly. "That they were," I agreed again.

She touched the greenhouse and peeked inside. "Is this where you grew all the flowers you gave out on the show?"

I could take a hint. I hurried over and cut her a long-stem peach-colored rose, her favorite.

"A rose for the beautiful lady." I handed it to her carefully so she could avoid the thorns.

She burst into a smile as she took it, bringing it to her nose. "You remembered!"

It was a bit unsettling that she thought I wouldn't, but she continued to smile. That was what mattered, especially after her rough beginning arriving here. "You can come out anytime and get as many flowers as you want."

I watched her as I made that offer. It didn't land as well as I thought it would. Her facial expression didn't change. She didn't even look up from the rose. She seemed to care more about me remembering which color rose she liked than to have access to all the live plants. Maybe she really didn't like nature that much. Or, maybe, more likely, she was tired from all the traveling.

"I hope you're okay with staying in the guesthouse until we are married?"

Her blues eyes flicked to me. "What?"

"I promised my daughter she wouldn't have to have any uncomfortable conversations with my granddaughters."

We stood silent, looking at each other. Clouds passing in the sky had taken the high temperature with them, making the heat much more comfortable.

"Oh," she said.

"Mags, we're still getting to know each other. I don't want to rush us. You."

"Oh."

I cleared the lump in my throat. This was harder than I thought it would be. I wasn't sure what she had been expecting. We probably should have talked about this before. "You okay with that for at least now?"

She looked up from her twisting fingers. "Furnished?"

"Yes."

She looked back down at her fingers that were still in a jumble. The silence between us seem to draw out until at last, she said, "Where's all my furniture going to go?"

I sighed, relieved. "There are lots of places that buy furniture. You aren't going to need it. Or, there's the garage."

She stared at me, eyes wide.

This moving in together was more awkward than I had anticipated. "Garage it is."

CHAPTER 3

M aggie

THE SUN WAS STILL UNBEARABLY hot when JT and I stepped outside to tackle the rest of the unloading. The time we had taken for the tour of the house had lowered the temperature maybe three or four degrees. So, it was only 114 or 115 degrees instead of 118. Almost tolerable. Plus, we'd been refreshed by guzzling down two water bottles each.

JT took large determined steps in his cowboy boots. "Let's get 'er done."

I scurried after him, looking every which way for the returning snake, a new one, or some other reptile surprise. I now knew they could be lurking on these grass-free lawns.

"Do you like not having grass?" I called out to JT.

He continued repositioning boxes. "It's low mainte-nance, which is perfect for me."

He didn't think about the pleasure of stepping bare foot on long thick green grass, or the allure of a well-manicured lawn. No, he thought in terms of upkeep. I hoped he didn't think about women that way. If he did, I'd soon be in trouble.

My brow wrinkled, staring at a yard full of rocks and large trees with pokey cacti here and there—everything brown and mostly dirt—with an occasional mute green. This landscape was very unappealing.

"Remember the Rocky Mountains?" We had spent a couple of days with them thundering around us while we filmed in Idaho.

He hefted two large boxes in his arms. "Well, the Rockies are pretty, too, but this is desert country and water is scarce."

The man was practical. Had to give him that.

It must have shown that I didn't completely buy that argument because he added, "This place is full of beauty, but you have to want to see it. It's there. It's unique."

I hurried up the ramp, bouncing, my ankle not hurting as much. I picked up two light boxes, determined to carrying my weight on this job. Wanting to put on a good face, I added, "I look forward to being able to see it."

"You won't regret it. The Sonoran Desert is a living landscape with more than two thousand different plants. You'll find a lot more life here in this region than you would ever see in California. This is a special place."

I decided I would just have to trust him on that because I had no interest in wandering outside more than the front yard to go hunting for those plants. I was sure the landscape held a lot of animals and insects, too. In an effort to avoid the lecture on that, though, I opted to watch JT carry large loads to the guesthouse. He piled the heavy boxes on top of one another and strolled off the trailer like it was no big deal. The way his muscles bulged underneath the T-shirt was sexy. That, I could watch every day.

It took less than a half hour to carry the boxes to the guesthouse. All that remained was my super-duper heavy, solid oak armoire. JT stood at the end of the trailer and stared at it, jaw drawn even tighter as a bead of sweat race down into his rugged beard.

I strode up and stood at his side. "Hey, baby, how about we go knock on the neighbor's door and ask if there's a man of the house who would be willing to help us out?"

"We don't need it. Hop out." He gestured for me to move out of the trailer.

He jumped out of the trailer and offered me a hand, which I took as I squatted down to climb off. He hooked his arms around my legs and swung me to the ground.

I yelped.

He set me on my feet, then pulled up the ramp. Before I recovered from the shock of him lifting me, he jumped into the driver's seat of his truck. I scurried to the passenger side of the truck to not be left behind.

With his gaze fixed on the side mirror, occasionally flicking with purpose to the rearview, he whipped the truck and trailer up onto the driveway in front of the garage door in no time flat. The man made things happen. That was attractive.

As he shifted the truck into park, I clapped.

His gaze slid my way with a questioning expression. "All I did was back up."

"But it was impressive." I quirked up one side of my mouth. "You just did it with no hemming or hawing."

He shook his head like I was being silly, which I was, mostly. I did manage to squeeze a slight smile out of him.

"See, we don't need help." He shoved open his truck door.

"I see." I tumbled out of my side of the truck. "Now, we only need to haul the eight-hundred-pound thing a hundred feet instead of nine hundred. So much easier."

He looked back where the truck had been to verify his calculation. "That's only six hundred feet. Much easier."

We regrouped at the back of the trailer and peered into its dim depths. The armoire hunkered there, looking stubborn.

"How much did you say it weighs?"

I shrugged. "I really don't know, but I'm guessing eight hundred and fifty. It gained a couple pounds sitting there."

JT shoved his cowboy hat back a few inches and rubbed his forehead with the heel of his hand.

"Got a plan?" I asked.

"Thinking."

"We could go knock on the—"

"Give me a few minutes and I'll figure it out."

The orange sun lowered, creating an additional break in the heat. It would be better if he broke his back when it was less hot outside. He would be less uncomfortable when the furniture tumbled down on him and squished him like a dead fly.

"JT, doing this by yourself is crazy. Seriously, I could

call the Mormon Missionaries. I'm sure we could have a whole crew here within an hour or two. It would be better than you hurting yourself."

His jaw drew tight again. "Other people create chaos."

I gulped. That didn't go over well. "But I don't want you to hurt your back, and I don't want to hurt mine."

"I never said anything about *you* doing anything." His face flushed. "Why don't you go make yourself a cup of tea?"

I stared at him. There was something in his voice. I wasn't sure what it was, but it was hard and unyielding, the sort of quality that made CEOs successful and most people obey.

Not me.

I shivered in the heat as we glared at each other. The man was committed to doing things a certain way. I could see that.

Earlier I'd taken note of the stacks of light-green tinted plastic containers in the garage. The foot-high boxes stacked onto each other and precise black writing labeling the contents. Moving furniture would be no less controlled. Come hell or high water, he would manage the armoire the way he wanted.

Fine, two could play that game. Come hell or high water, we would do it *together*.

"JT, I don't know what's going on here, but I don't really like it. That armoire cannot be frightened into coming into the house no matter how much you glare at it, and I can't be ordered away like one of your people."

For a second, his demeanor blackened even more. The lowering sun shone over his shoulders, almost blinding me, and turning him into a dark, two-dimensional silhou-ette of a person. His face was all shadow.

The stifling heat separated us from each other and everything. Sweat clung to his shirt, outlining his strength. He tipped his head back and blew out a long breath. His cowboy hat tumbled to the ground. Bending over to pick it up, his dim face held a rueful smile.

"Sorry, I'm not used to people giving me suggestions."

"Helping you, JT. I was helping. Or trying to."

He reached up and tugged me forward a few steps into his arms. "I've lived by myself for a long time."

I curled up on his chest, feeling his sweat, his strength, his love. I closed my eyes, again at home in his arms. A few minutes later, he shifted his weight and I looked up. "What do you do when you need help?" I spoke softly, hoping to not cause him to bolt.

He shrugged with a flash of heaviness in his eyes. "Just get along."

"That must be extremely lonely."

He shrugged like he was trying to shake that off, but I saw him swallow.

I sighed, my forehead wrinkling in concern. "From now on, we work as a team, right?"

He went as still as a block of ice in my arms. Then, as if melted by the sun, he dropped a swift kiss on my lips and released me. He backed up, eyeing the truck. "Ri-i-ight," he said slowly, like he wasn't convinced. He gave the armoire a dirty look.

I guess that was what the team was doing—giving menacing glares to furniture—so I joined in. What a team of glarers.

"Okay, I have an idea," he said. "Ready?"

I rubbed my hands. "Pitch it here."

"Let's do it this way. Why don't you go to the far end of the truck and…"

I did as he directed, vaguely unsettled and almost reassured by the kiss on the lips.

"Is here good?" I called out, shifting my weight on the cement floor, stained to look like marble.

"Yes," he called back to me as he went deeper into the garage. He had found a long flat thing with wheels on it. Apparently, he was still figuring out how to move an eight-hundred-pound piece of furniture by himself. For being so rich, he was certainly unwilling to use his money to solve solutions.

"You can go inside if you like. I have this handled."

I crossed my arms across my chest even though he wasn't watching. "I am going to stay right here and watch you accomplish this feat."

He looked back at me with a shake of his head and a sly smile.

I waved my arms with pretend pom poms. "Go, JT!" I wiggled my butt for extra emphasis.

JT laughed quietly at my cheerleading performance. A spark returned to his eyes. Feeling encouraged, I hurried up the ramp and watched him plant the flat boards with wheels down in front of the armoire.

"It's a furniture dolly," he said. "One of my craftsmen designs and manufactures them."

He spread out the boards on the bottom of the trailer, then stood on tiptoes to push the armoire onto them. His muscles strained and bulged as his face turned a deep red.

He shifted in a flash to holding the piece against his back, looking like he was performing a Herculean feat.

He sank under the weight of the piece and gasped, "Put a dolly under the back corners."

I stared at his pouring beads of sweat, and down to the corner of the armoire where he wanted me to crawl and secure the dolly.

"One on each side."

He had to be kidding. He wanted me to crawl under the eight-hundred-pound armoire and trust he would keep it from crushing me?

"Hurry." His voice had lowered several octaves.

I frantically scanned the trailer for the dollies. "Where are they?"

"Far left corner."

I grabbed them and, with slippery hands, rushed them under the armoire. My back hurt from squatting so low, and my thighs screamed. Today's workout was becoming too much. I might have to do my regular yoga class more often.

"There," I yelled as I hurried out.

He lowered the furniture onto the dollies and held the other end, his face redder than a fire truck. "Great. Slip the other two under this end."

I did what he said. It seemed to work out well. We continued to work together, getting that enormous thing down the ramp and into the garage. My heart pounded and my breath rattled as we eased the mammoth piece of furniture to its feet.

I wiped my arm over my forehead and, between gasps, smiled at JT. "We're a good team."

He rubbed his gloved hands together, gaze locking onto mine. He strolled over to me to hook his arms around my neck and pull me to him, smelling every bit of a man. He kissed the top of my forehead. "That we are."

* * *

To RELAX, I flopped on top of the bulky green couch that tried to swallow me whole. The six-hundred-foot guest cottage sported tan tile floors and cumbersome southwestern rugs in native medallion designs tossed at random to soften the hardness of the floor. Overlooking the rugs, on the left wall, hung the skull of a steer with feather accents dangling from its horns. But that didn't even compete with the animal skin pinned above the brick fireplace with a decorative mandala pattern painted onto the leather.

I scooted deeper into the couch. I would have never figured JT to be a guy to decorate with a dead Bambi like it was a trophy. He seemed too soft-hearted. But here I was in a museum of death with carcasses used as art. I shuddered as I peeked at the skull one more time. That thing should be buried, not hung on a wall. Sorry, Georgia O'Keeffe.

My phone rang its classical Mozart, in sharp contrast to the quiet in my room. I snatched my cell and clamped it to my ear. "Hello?"

"How's the move going?"

Dee. I closed my eyes in an effort to give me the strength to deal with this woman. The production manager from *Millionaire Engagement* was as ruthless as they came. I opened my eyes, ready for battle.

"Fine. Why?" One must always search for the underlying subtext of manipulation and thick clouds of the agenda when dealing with her. She was the very definition of shifty.

"Well, we here at *Millionaire Engagement* like to check-in with our former contestants and see how everything is going. We consider you one of the family."

Leaning against the couch, I rested my head on the back cushion, hoping to ease the pain in my neck. JT wasn't going to like that she called me, either. He was protective that way. I would have to tell him. I didn't want to be one of those couples who kept secrets from each other. "What do you want?"

"Didn't we agree to become friends? Isn't this what friends do?"

I didn't agree to that. I would most certainly remember. She was as much of a snake as the reptile JT had just thrown into the backyard. She was sneaky and could strike at the most unexpected times, and a tall brick wall wouldn't be enough to keep her away. To say I agreed to be friends with her was either a lie to butter me up, or she had confused me with another contestant. Maybe the star of the last season, Charissa. Making friends with Dee seemed Charissa's style.

But telling a snake I didn't trust her wasn't a great idea.

"If you want to be friends, we can be friends. We just finished unloading all my stuff into JT's guesthouse. Why don't you swing by and help me unpack?"

"You aren't staying in the same house?"

Really? Don't answer my question and go for the soft spot. Typical. Heat flushed my face. "JT is traditional. You know that."

A sounded banged in the background through the phone. She must be calling from an office. "Yeah, well, that's getting extreme. So, have you two set a date yet?"

Boom, there it was. As much as I didn't like Dee, and as much as I was certain we were two totally different people... I wondered the same thing. On the move here I'd asked about our wedding date. All JT said was, "We have lots of time." Well, sure, if you were throwing rattlesnakes over the back fence, one might think of time differently, but I had left my life for this snake-infested place. I needed reassurance. I needed a ring on my finger.

Dee wanted the publicity. The season of reality TV I starred in ended with JT proposing to Milly instead of me. Me winning him back off camera had been big news, but they didn't shoot that because JT protected me from the media. According to JT, the media had ruined his and Milly's relationship. I wasn't going to let that happen to us. Television reporters had also cast me as the villain through the magic of editing. I had made it too easy for Dee to do that by not keeping up my guard with her. I wasn't going to make that mistake again.

The show wanted to watch the villain—me—and the super-rich cowboy—JT—glide down the aisle. They wanted to unearth how I cast a black magic love potion to make him fall in love with me. After all, the only reason JT would fall in love with me and leave the sweet Milly was the fact I was a witch. The world, no matter how evolved it thought it was, wasn't. Powerful women were still witches and burned at the stake, either literally or through social media scorn.

I wasn't opposed to having the date locked down, although being aligned with Dee was unsettling. "JT and I could try to come up with a date. I would have to talk to him."

She sighed. "As you know, *Millionaire Engagement* is not only about making great TV and getting high ratings, and we have done both of those. But one of our core missions is to show that older people can find love. Not only can they do that, but they can do it better than younger people because they have more maturity. Since you two were in our first season and are the classic example of the type of message we want to send to the public, we'd like you to spread that message."

I closed my eyes. It was like she wanted us to be the salespeople and preach the gospel of *Millionaire Engagement*. The show that had cast me as a villain. The first few months after the airing, I was spit on, not served at restaurants, and watched heads shake in disgust when I passed by.

Dee continued, "As you remember, in the terms of the contract, we'll cover all the costs of the wedding ceremony. We'll decorate and perform it exactly the way you want it, no cost spared. And, you can have as many of your friends and loved ones as you want. We'd shoot the wedding live on national TV."

JT hadn't mentioned one word about marriage. Not one. Not a hint. Nothing.

"We thought it'd be a great pre-show to the next season, so we'd need to shoot in a month in Sedona, which is the best place in the United States for a wedding. We already have contracts lined up. Don't worry, it'll be stunning."

That was soon. Sedona? I had never been there. Only heard about it in New Age circles in LA. I sat up straighter on the sofa, staring at the brush outside my window. A tumbleweed blew by. Sedona had red mountains, upscale restaurants, paved sidewalks, dress shops, and vortexes.

Dee kept chugging on. "We'd prefer that Anna and Lexi, JT's granddaughters, be involved somehow in the wedding. They are certainly the public's favorites."

Unlike me. I heard the pounding of my heart knocking against my rib cage. Dee was selling the fairytale wedding with red rocks and vortexes and happy fans.

She stopped talking, drawing out the anticipation with a long, pregnant pause. Dee whispered loudly, "What do you say?"

I sat in a room with skulls on the wall, while snakes slithering around outside, and 118-degree scorched the earth. I missed JT.

Dee continued, "That must be scary to be dependent on a man for everything when you aren't even sure you'll tie the knot."

Nice one, planting doubt. I straightened my back. "Not scary at all. We love each other, and this time I'm with a good guy."

She cleared her throat. "That's what Milly said, too, but I guess *you* and JT are different. I'm sure you know how to keep your man."

A shadow flickered on the rustic southwestern lodge rug. Catch men, yes. Keep them? I swallowed a lump in my throat. My track record wasn't exceptional on that front.

"Listen, Dee, we've agreed to have you film the wedding, and as soon as we have a date, we'll let you know."

"When do you think you can do it?"

This wasn't about TV anymore. This was about me and JT. And Dee didn't have a role in that. I sat back and looked at the cow skull. "Look, Dee, I appreciate your interest in our happily ever after. As I just said, you'll be one of the first to know. Until then, I'm not playing this game." The day had transformed to a pale light of dusk. I hung up the phone.

I had stood up to "The Great Dee." I had actually done it. I paced the darkening room, heart thumping in excitement, not believing I called her on her game. She tried to play me and I had none of it. I brushed at a hair that fell across my face. No one and nothing was going to come between me and JT if I could help it, even if I was surrounded by cow skulls and tumbleweeds.

I flicked on the overhead light. Dee had been tricky tempting me with the glitz and glam world, but I didn't fall for it this time. Nope. I chose JT and me as a team. I was on his team and he was on mine, far away from the prying eyes of television. I'd find a way to make it work in his world with biting cactus, wandering coyotes, and yard-less houses. Whatever it took. We were going to have an epic romance.

To continue to make this life mine, I looked over at the lumpy, shadowy boxes. I'd start with them. I picked up one of them and wandered into the small, but beautiful, bathroom and admired the sail tiles decorating the walls. I opened the rich, heavy oak cabinet's drawer and found a fluffy pink plastic package of pads and tampons.

What?

I tugged opened the drawers next to the sink cabinet to find a half bottle of perfume, a used purple toothbrush, and half-used toothpaste.

Had to be Milly's. It would figure as she was confined to the cottage, too.

At least we were even on that score.

From what I knew about her and JT's break up, which didn't include many of the juicy details, it had ended abruptly. She must have left the stuff in haste, in an upset, from absent mindedness, or… actually, I didn't care.

This problem would be simple to solve. I snatched the small copper trash can and dumped all of Milly's remnants into it, then hurried to the house to seek out JT for comfort. I needed his strength wrapped around me to encourage me to adjust, and reassure me we were on the same page.

The glass back door opened with ease, and I stepped into his empty kitchen. "Hello?" I called out into the large southwestern house. There was a glass of water on the black granite countertop and a few pieces of mail, mostly bills. They hadn't been there the last time I was in the room, so JT must be catching up.

My stomach twisted, and my breath came out strangled. I shouldn't be nervous finding JT in his own home. I was his fiancée. Still, my stomach twisted in more knots. In truth, we hadn't spent a ton of time alone together, but that didn't mean I didn't love him. I did. Despite that, I had no idea how he would respond to his personal space being invaded.

Tentatively, I called out, "JT?"

He wasn't in the front room or the living room, but fumbling noises flittered from the bedroom. A few moments later, his head popped out. "Yes?"

Even with ruffled hair and sleep in his eyes, he was as attractive as ever with his rugged looks. My breath caught before I caved into my impulse and rushed up to him. I curled up into his welcoming arms and closed my eyes, breathing in his closeness and our connection as he cradled me with affection. I felt his love, his strength, and it calmed me as he softly stroked my back.

"When are we going to dinner?" I purred in his arms.

He stepped back to give my question some thought. He rubbed his hands through his hair. "I think I still have a can of soup in the cupboard."

Soup? From a can? He had to be kidding about eating canned soup. Right? He didn't look like he starved, and we had worked hard all day. He must be as starved as I was.

"I'm hungry."

"BBQ? We could do ribs."

The spread of the antlers on the far wall caught my eye. I would never ask, but there was a chance he killed and skinned the meat to that animal. We could be eating the remains. I swallowed hard. "Um, it's pretty hot for a lot of meat… let's go out."

His eyes grew large. "You want to eat out? You don't want to stay home and just have a relaxing time together?"

His eyes studied me for a long, drawn-out time as my nerves kicked in. He didn't want to go out to eat. The man was serious about soup… more than going somewhere nice. He was much more of a homebody than I ever took him for.

His brow crinkled.

I swallowed a huge lump that manifested in my throat.

He liked home cooking.

We were in trouble.

I never mastered that skill beyond reading directions from boxes and dumping things into boiling water. If he wanted me to cook for him, I'd do that. He had, after all, done so much for me but, after eating a couple rounds of my meals, he might have second thoughts about us. My chest tightened. It looked like I was going to have to figure out how to cook.

I headed to the first cupboard by the sliding glass door. I opened the cupboard door to find an entire shelf of cookbooks, including Betty Crocker, and others about using the crockpot and grill. I pulled one cookbook out and flipped it open. Feminine writing sprawled on the side of this recipe and that recipe. His wife's. She did cook and, apparently, complicated dishes.

The presence of other women filled this house. First, Milly's toiletries. Now Irene's cookbooks. My heart pounded.

I looked over to JT. How was he handling me searching his wife's cupboard? "Is this okay?"

His expression grew blank. "It's your home now."

I looked back at the books, then to him. My stomach clenched into a tight knot. This was a tricky situation. I loved my man, and I wanted to respect his past. My finger lingered on the cookbook. I didn't want to hurt him.

"Go ahead," he said as though guessing at what I wanted to do.

I looked back at him. He nodded toward the cookbooks. "They are yours now. Do what you want."

I gulped. That was kind of him. This couldn't be easy. It wasn't like it was a breakup where there was a lot of bad feelings between them. He had loved her. He had married her. He had been by her side until she passed away, but I needed my place in this house if we were going to work. I pulled out another cookbook, feeling its weight. I set it on the counter.

JT gave a nod, his face pale, jaw set firm. I pulled out a stack of old-fashioned cookbooks and put them on the counter. It didn't take long for me to clear all the ones I could reach. I grabbed a chair and climbed onto it to reach more books. As the stack grew, the books slid until the entire counter on the right side of the sink was covered by them.

Sweat dotted my forehead, I stepped off the chair and walked out of the sliding door to grab moving boxes. When I came back into the kitchen, JT stood there with a coffee mug in his hand. Not drinking, just standing there. My heart pounded even harder.

"You okay?"

He nodded.

"It's got to be weird having a new woman move into Irene's domain."

He took a sip of coffee. "I want you to be here with me."

I flashed a glance at him. He was handling this well. Much better than I would have or, in fact, was. Despite that this had to be hard on him, I still couldn't help but feel like I was being compared to another woman who had been okay with real rattlesnakes, 118-degree weather, antlers, and doing the cooking.

JT set his coffee mug on the counter with a thud, strolled over, and stacked the cookbooks into boxes. "I'll take those."

The last thing I wanted to do was display my jealousy over a person who had passed away, or be insensitive. "Okay." If he was willing to pack them away, I wasn't going to stop him.

Once all the books were in the boxes, I found a quarter loaf of wheat bread in the cupboard and plopped the limp bag onto the counter.

From the next cupboard, I grabbed two brown bowls that clicked together when I set them by the bread. Continuing to open doors, I snatched up the garlic, onion, and parsley spices and two boxes of leaf tea—chamomile to settle my stomach and an assortment of sweet teas to please him.

The last cupboard—the pantry—I opened to find a shelf with a few packages and cans lined up in perfect order toward the back. Not scattered in true bachelor fashion, but exactly a half inch left between the rows. Each can faced exactly straight toward me.

"You sure do like order," I muttered.

"It makes life simpler," he said.

I had never seen anything like it before, except in the movies. I nodded to his comment. Order brought ease. I would have to remember that. I browsed through the cans and selected a stew.

I held the soup above my head, waving it to see if it would meet JT's approval for dinner. He pointed to a drawer by the stove to let me know where to find the can opener. As I opened the stew, he pulled out a saucepan. I emptied the soup in it, turned on the stove, and hunted for rice. I found instant rice, which would work perfectly. Ten minutes later, we sat at the dining table, rice at the bottom of our bowls and stew on top, with buttered toast and steaming tea.

JT smiled. "I never had rice with stew before. What a great idea." He dug in with enthusiasm.

I stared at my stew. This was my new life. My chest tightened. This was so pedestrian.

We ate in silence for several minutes. I lowered my spoon. "Are you upset about me clearing the cupboard?"

He stopped eating, spoon midway to his mouth and shook his head no. "It's time."

"I don't want you thinking that I'm trying to erase your wife."

"Don't worry about it."

But worrying about it was exactly what I did throughout the rest of the meal. Neither of us said a word. Me, because I didn't know really how to fit in this world. I had just emptied three shelves of his wife's cookbooks. Him, I didn't know what was going on with him, but he didn't have his "CEO" on—the problem-solving, go-get-'em look. He looked… tired and sad. Very sad.

I paused, holding my last spoonful of salty canned stew, and stared at JT and his morose manner. How often had he sat here with his late wife? How often did he eat her soup —her homemade cooked-with-love soup? How did he feel about *this* soup? About the fact that he'd just moved his late wife's cookbooks for me. How did he feel about *me?*

His eyes lifted to mine. We looked at each for a long moment before his face softened and he put down his spoon. He came around the table to hug me. "Let's go."

I was so confused. "Where?"

"To drop off cookbooks at Goodwill."

My throat thickened with emotion, "Oh." I certainly hadn't expected that.

"And to get you a hot tub."

I gasped with surprise, reached up to him, and pulled him down for a passionate kiss. "Thank you," I whispered.

Several minutes later, we slipped into one of his sports cars with the radio playing classical music softly in the background. The low hum of the air conditioner struggled to beat down the oppressive heat. The musical notes rang pure and crisp. The melody stole my breath and sunk deep into me, vibrating with my spirit.

I closed my eyes and let the music engulf me as I settled into one of the most comfortable leather seats I had ever experienced. The cushions immersed me in luxury.

"Wow, this is nice. I never realized the extravagance of driving a sports car. I thought it was all about status and driving fast. I didn't know it could transform one's soul."

JT's whole face lit up. "That it can."

He liked me appreciating his car. I blinked before peering out the window at Tucson in the dusk. The cactus matched well with the pastel colors in the sky. Maybe Tucson wasn't as bad as I thought. I reached over and rubbed his neck as he leaned into my touch. "Thank you."

His shoulders relaxed as he slowed the car for a red light.

* * *

JT

Watching Maggie clean out Irene's cooking shelf pierced me in the heart, making it hard for air to squeeze in or out of my lungs. Maggie was beautiful with the last of the day's light reflecting in her shining blond hair, but I hadn't opened that cupboard once since Irene passed. It had her fingerprints all over it: cookbooks with bookmarks and papers stuffed in them, and rugged and torn covers showing the wear and tear of much use. I couldn't look. It brought up too many mixed feelings. My relationship had been complicated in its simple way. I loved her, but not like I felt with Maggie.

Irene had always been there. She took care of the house and our child and fed me. With Maggie I felt young, alive, and she made me smile and laugh a lot. Two very different women. Two very different relationships. I wasn't sure what it would look like with Maggie, but I had a sense it was going to be filled with a lot more adventures.

She had sure been a trouper today with the heat, the cactus, and a snake. Her face flushed as she opened the cookbook to see Irene's purple writing. It forced her to confront the reality of my past, and the fact I still had Irene in the house. I should have put that stuff away before she came here.

I watched as she took down book after book from the shelf. All those books. All those meals. All those memories. Irene had pored over those recipes as though they held the secrets of the universe. My finger twitched at my side, but other than that, I didn't move as I watched my new love remove the mark of my old. The coffee mug grew heavy in my hand.

When one of the books crashed to the ground, it snapped me into action. I needed to protect those books, those confusing memories. When Maggie left, I put my mug on the counter and rushed to the books and stacked them straight. Irene would have been mad about the books being out of order, but I never knew her system. Before I could give it any more thought, Maggie was back with moving boxes. I started sorting them into the cardboard containers.

The moment she turned her attention to the next cupboard, I hefted the box in my arms to store Irene's cookbooks someplace out of sight. She didn't need to have them in her face. Plus, she needed room in the kitchen for her things. I understood that, but I doubted she'd understand why I was still holding onto some of Irene's books. I would let the box of less-used books go to Goodwill as a gesture to Maggie of my love for her.

Later, Maggie hunched over her soup like she lacked the energy to sit straight. Her narrowed eyes wrinkled at the corners, and her mouth stretched tight into an upsetting frown.

I shifted in my seat. I needed to say something to either lessen the frown or make it slightly better. But what could I say? As the result of the pressure, I stared at the salt and pepper shakers in the middle of the table and her frown lines deepened.

We needed a change of focus fast. I would have to take her to buy a hot tub despite how dreadfully tired I was.

That would put a smile back on her face and help her to become more comfortable with her new life.

When I told her where we were going, a smile came, and she was back on my arm talking at her normal fast clip. It was nice to note she could recover fast and let issues fall away. That was going to make things easier. We approached the hot tub store near closing time.

I flipped the keys in my hand. "Let's make this fast." I have never been one for shopping. Weariness made my eyelids heavier with each passing moment, but easing her transition into my life would be worth it.

"Are you achy, baby?" Maggie hooked her arm in mine and, for a second, rested her head on my shoulder. She felt right on my arm, and like we were a team once more. This had been a good idea. Right before we reached the glass doors, she stopped, staring at the sign in the far corner.

"It says no guns allowed." She looked up at me with those big eyes of hers, wide and full of apprehension. "Is gun carrying so common here that they have to… post signs?" Her voice broke and her happiness faded again.

"You're safe." I rubbed her forearm to reassure her.

"But people carry guns?"

I shrugged, playing it down even though I could tell it was hard for her to wrap her mind around such behavior. "It keeps people safe." I nudged her to keep going into the store. I needed to distract her from the subject before she freaked out. "Come on, there isn't much time until the place closes, and you still want a hot tub, right?"

She fell back in step with me but grew quiet. I could almost see her thinking about how different everything was from California. She acted like this was the final frontier, and there were wild cowboys on every corner who would shoot at random.

"Statistically it's much safer here than in California. It might take time to get used to things here. You'll learn to love it."

She pressed her lips together, and turned a bit pale. "Looking forward to it," she said as she stepped into the shop.

The place was spread out with tubs every couple of feet on a tile floor. The décor was nonexistent. A lady dressed in slacks and blouse with extremely short blue hair strolled up to us.

She forced a smile. "How can I help you?"

"A hot tub?" Maggie gave me a double take as though she wasn't sure.

I nodded in agreement.

The lady looked between us as though she was trying to figure out our dynamics. "What's the criteria?"

I cleared my throat, too tired to think. This was Maggie's department, but she wasn't saying anything.

"Cost? Size? Shape?" The sales lady offered to get us going.

Maggie almost cowered away from the woman. Her lips drew taut, and she stood there stiffly, almost like a human mannequin. It took me a moment to figure out that she was shy about spending my money.

"Pick what makes you happy. Whatever you want," I offered.

That was all she needed to hear. With the freedom not to worry about the cost, she tucked her hand back into the crook of my arm. We wandered around the store, the sales clerk trailing behind us. Maggie took the lead and I followed until she stopped and peeked at a price tag. She gasped. "This is expensive. I don't have to have one."

The sales lady placed one hand on the tub frame. "Ready to get rid of the aches at the end of the day? You and your man…"

"That sounds nice." Maggie peered back at me with a shy smile. She turned again to the store clerk, but her face abruptly fell into a concerned expression. "You seem like you could use a dunk in a tub," Maggie said to the employee.

To my horror, the salesclerk burst out in tears. She wiped at them and tried to blink them away and sniffed, but her efforts to stop the emotional flood didn't work.

She leaned in to the woman. "Tell me… what's the matter?"

Maggie looked angelic as she laid a hand on the woman's arm. My insides fluttered. Nothing was more attractive than a kind woman, aware of others. My fiancée was probably as exhausted as I was, but she found the energy to recognize another's trouble and offer compassion. Underneath everything, Maggie had a good heart.

She leaned in closer to the lady and spoke in a low tone, probably so a lurking boss wouldn't hear. "It has to be a guy or a child."

The saleslady looked around and wiped running mascara from her cheek. "A guy." The way she broke into sobs made my stomach twist.

Maggie sighed. "That is so painful."

The lady sniffed. "It really is. No one really prepares you." The lady twisted her fingers and glanced at me with red eyes and the pain from her personal trauma felt palpable. Her expression told me she really wanted to be left alone with Maggie to talk. I happily obliged the unexpressed wish, as Maggie had a good grasp on the situation. She freaked out and trembled at a mere sight of a snake, but spot a troubled woman with man issues and she dove right in to help. It came as a natural thing for her, like breathing.

I strolled through the store pretending to study hot tubs and their product descriptions while Maggie and the salesclerk huddled in their own world. Glad to focus on something else, I learned there were a lot more options to hot tubs than cell towers. This industry had gone hog wild on catering to preferences—oval, square, round, triangle. I even saw one that could hang over a fire and sit in like a cauldron to become somebody's dinner.

I made it halfway across the room, peering at tub after tub, when Maggie's laughter filled the store. The bubbling rhythm of her storytelling sounded uplifting even though I could not make out what she was saying. I liked hearing her happy. She had a great laugh and it seem to help others, too.

I glanced at my watch. We had to get going—it had to be near closing time. Maggie could connect with the clerk tomorrow for coffee or shopping or whatever women did when they were friends.

As I approached, Maggie leaned toward the clerk, talking with an intensity and with a spark I had been hoping to see all day.

The salesclerk gestured to Maggie. "You have one smart lady here. I hope you appreciate her."

I smiled. "I'm a lucky man to have her in my life. She might not be good with snakes, but she works magic with soup cans."

Maggie faked elbowed me in my torso. "That wasn't nice. There was a snake on our front yard today."

The store clerk's eyes got wide. "Diamondback or Mojave?"

"What?" Maggie asked. Her eyebrows pinched together.

I laughed. "Diamondback."

The store clerk nodded. "Those are scary to come across."

I hooked my arm around Maggie's neck and drew her close to me and kissed her on the top of her forehead. "Mag, I hate to break up the party, but the store closes in ten minutes and we need to make a decision."

The store clerk wiped at her eyes and squared her shoulders. "Oh, sorry." She flushed. "Do you want recreational or therapeutic?"

Maggie moved her eyebrows up and down in an extremely suggestive manner and whispered in my ear, "I think no matter which tub we get, we can make it both. What do you think?"

I flushed, unsure how to respond to that in public. Maggie's apparent intention was to make it a game to tease me and make sleeping in separate beds hard.

Maggie laughed. She swiveled to the salesclerk. "Let's start with recreational."

The woman straightened up and wiped the last tears from her eyelashes. "Two people? Four? Six?"

I waited for Maggie to do her thing. This was her

present. She needed to get what she wanted as long as it wasn't the cauldron or shocking pink.

Maggie looked up at me. "Are you wanting a tub just for us to enjoy the sunsets, or are you going to want to invite your daughter and her husband and kids along?"

How cool of her to think of my daughter and granddaughter. I had never given them a thought in relation to a jacuzzi, but it would be something both would enjoy. "Good point. Six." I reached out and squeezed her hand. "That's a good point. Really good."

Our saleswoman led us back to the options with those specifications and she brightened with the possibility of a bigger commission. To the left sat a large oval hot tub with dark tan tile.

Maggie drifted over to it and glanced at the price. Her eyes bulged. "That sucker is expensive—really expensive."

The money seemed to be getting to her. My world was a whole new one. "Do you like it?"

She looked flustered. I could tell she wanted to protest because of the cost, but also wanted the tub.

"What do you think?" she asked to avoid my question.

"I think I want to make you happy. Will it make you happy?"

She flushed again. "Being with you makes me happy."

That was the right answer. "Then, I'm happy." I flopped out my credit card. "Let's get this done. We need to go."

"If eating canned soup and buying hot tubs is what it takes to keep my guy happy, I've struck gold." Maggie smiled bashfully up at me.

"Wanna go for a walk in the moonlight?"

CHAPTER 4

*M*aggie

THE NIGHT WAS pitch black except for the extreme pale yellow light that mutely reflected from JT's cell phone. I struggled to gulp down my ragged breaths and waves of panic. In contrast, JT relaxed in the darkness, shoulders lowered, and his gait slowed to a leisurely stroll.

I shivered under the absolute stillness.

My eyes stayed glued to the road before me. With every step, I made sure the blacktop was clear of creepy crawly things. Rarely did I see any live thing, but one had to be careful. The unnerving part of focusing so intently on the street was that it might keep me from seeing any signs of dangerous animals hiding under the blanket of nightfall. They had to be there with hungry bellies urging them to scavenge for food, human or otherwise. I had seen so many in just this one day: a snake, coyote, squirrels, bunnies, and a ton of birds, including a hawk. I kept my ears perked for the rustling sound of predators drawing close.

Breathing deeply, I told myself I could survive this. JT was with me. He'd protect me. He'd know what to do. And somehow, he found peace in this clean air and wide-open land. I doubted there was any way I could become comfortable with this…this nature JT loved. Maybe I could make a life staying indoors when he felt the urge to wander outside. I could be the loving arms he returned to. My crossed arms tightened around my chest. Was that a hoot of an owl?

"What's that?" My voice cracked as I scooted closer to JT.

He pulled on my clasped forearm, clearly wanting to grasp my hand. I resisted, not sure if I could let go of the comfort my folded arms provided, protecting me against the daunting moonlit evening and all its cover concealed.

"Come on." He tugged my arm until it released, and his hand swallowed my own. "It's an owl saying hi."

My fingers curled into his warm hand. "It's so dark, and there are so many animals lurking."

He pulled me closer to his side as he chuckled. "You're fine. Animals are good for the soul."

What was good for my soul was to be on my bed in the guesthouse, away from all the threats, with the door locked tight. I needed to be protected from all this wildness, not thrust into the middle of it and told it was good for me. I had been chased by too many angry dogs when I was little. Twice when I tried to make it by that neighbor's house, his large wolf-like dog bared its white fangs at me. When I started to run away, it barked at my retreating back, shooting pure panic down my spine. Many other times, friends' dogs had jumped and nipped at me with their bare fangs. Dogs have no sense of boundaries, and in the Wild West that was probably worse.

Though eating an apple a day might be good for me, even though allergies made my tongue swell up into a tennis ball, at least it contained vitamins. Being in the wild with creatures that can munch on humans was not good for anything. It troubled my soul. Being *safe* was good for my soul. Being thrust into the final frontier of the Wild West was extremely trying.

I said nothing. We continued to walk. Our footsteps sounded loud in contrast to the silence. Our feet crunched against rocks and dead leaves as we made our way around the neighborhood.

Finally, after we rounded a corner, houses appeared in the distance, which made me feel a little safer. The moon continued to pour down on us.

"Why did you let the snake go?"

JT tightened his grip on my hand. "This is his home. We're invading it."

"That makes sense." I kicked a rock. "I guess you really are a nice guy—really caring about animals, but it's still scary. You know it'll come back."

He gave my fingers a quick squeeze. "You'll be fine." There was amusement in his voice, like he found my reaction silly. At least it didn't sound like it intended to shame or ridicule.

"But the coyotes."

I couldn't help but think one would spring on me from the dark, deciding I would make a good snack. We stepped on the extra gravelly part of the road. Crunching noises sounded beneath our shoes.

JT cleared his throat. "They're more afraid of you, than you are of them."

"I doubt that," I said, before catching myself.

He stopped walking. I followed his lead and halted about two feet from him. Had he heard something? "What are you doing?" I whispered, my throat constricted.

He turned his ear up, listening. My heart thudded. I scooted closer to him. Anything could be hidden in the darkness. JT tucked his phone away and pulled me into his arms to rest his chin on top of my head like a headrest.

I curled into his warm, strong body. He smelled good, like a forest. I closed my eyes as I rested my cheek against his muscular chest, hearing the comforting beat of his heart. We stood there for a long time before he spoke. "Most of the animals specifically avoid humans. You're safe."

It felt so safe to be in his arms in this mystic blue moon-light. He was sturdy and strong, and there was something inside me, maybe the scared little girl, who wanted to snug up into his arms and believe him. Another part of me stiffened. The animals would be around even if he weren't. What would happen then? He couldn't always be there with me when animals lurked around every corner in the desert. If I was truly going to live here, make this place my home, I would have to somehow navigate coyotes, snakes, hawks, and all. I couldn't be confined to the house. Somehow the animals and I were going to have to co-exist.

I let out a big breath. If I would be reassured that the animals would respect my boundaries, things would be fine. I was more than willing to leave them alone, and I just needed for them to do the same in return.

"Do you believe me?" he asked softly.

I shrugged. I wanted to, but maybe that wasn't enough to make him happy.

"Coyotes are scaredy-cats. They'll run away from you. It's much safer here than going on a reality TV show and being framed as the villain."

I burrowed more deeply into his embrace. He caressed my hair, letting all my unresolved angst flow through me. His words made me feel good. He believed I wasn't that person the media made me out to be.

We stayed in the hug for a long time. Occasionally a hoot of an owl let us know it was watching out for us. The wink of the moon going behind intermittent cloud cover offered us privacy. JT ran his hands through my hair, causing goosebumps to run down my arms. Huge waves of love swept through me. I pulled slightly from his embrace to peer up to his face reflecting in gentle moonlight. I couldn't see his eyes, and I doubted he could see mine, but that didn't stop him from bending down to kiss me.

When our lips met, bolts of warmth shot through me. Somehow, I believed JT. He would keep me safe. He would protect me. I would be okay even if I was surrounded by unpredictable creatures in the Wild West, where they posted gun signs outside of restaurants and hot tub stores.

He pulled away from me and took my hand again. We moved silently in the moonlight. "This is your new home. You'll learn to love it."

I said nothing. What could I say? I loved this man. I knew he wanted me here, and I wanted to be with him.

Somehow, I was going to need to come to an agreement with this place.

In an abrupt change of direction, JT hauled me off the blacktop onto the rocky dirt land.

"Wha—" My heartbeat picked up as he plowed into wild terrain.

He released my hand, fumbling in his back pocket.

I stopped walking and watched him keep going. He continued up to a large brick wall rimming someone's backyard. It was about a foot higher than my head.

In a strained whisper, I asked, "What are you doing? This is someone's property."

The last thing I wanted to do on my first night in Tucson was to be caught trespassing. Clearly these neighbors believed in carrying guns—even their streets were named Gunshot, Buckshot, and Gun Sling.

With something in his hand, JT strolled up against the wall, stood on his tippy toes, and made smacking noises with his tongue.

"Don't you have your own horses?"

"I've known these horses since they were colts, and I always stop by to say hi."

That made sense, I guess. Stopping for horses, not neighbors. I stayed where I stood, at least five feet away. The evening had transformed into a thick navy blue with whimsical clouds streaming along in the sky. The nearly full moon peeked out from the branches of all the tall trees, making the setting look like a painting. An idyllic painting one would never see in California. A gentle breeze blew against us as the smell of clean air flooded my senses.

"Here, boy," JT called, waving what must have been a carrot in his hand.

"Are the neighbors happy about you feeding their animals?"

An owl hooted, and JT continued to signal to the horse. Suddenly a large brown nose showed up over the brick, and white teeth reflected in the moonlight as the horse ate noisily from JT's hand. When the large animal finished, JT stroked his long nose.

"Good boy," he whispered.

"You sure do love animals, don't you?"

JT made his way back to me. He seized my hand.

"Of course."

"That is how I know you are a good guy. I've heard animals are good judges of character."

JT pulled me close to him. "Thanks for being here with me."

We continued our walk back home, saying nothing more. Instead, we let the evening talk to us in its mysterious and wise way.

CHAPTER 5

 T

THE NEXT MORNING, I strolled to my office. The room had an unused, dank smell of an unoccupied building that sat too long on the market. Despite the smell, I set my keys down, glad to be here. I noted the familiar sight of my desk, computer, chair, and golf clubs that sat in the corner. Before I could open a window or air out the room, Dimitri brushed past me, filling the space with his whirlwind energy. "Tell me the truth. How is it with Maggie invading your home?"

I stepped around my business partner and pulled up the blinds to crank open the window. A stream of chilled morning air weaved in.

"Maggie's not adapting as well as I thought she would."

"High maintenance?"

That didn't really fit. More like she was a jittery bird. Afraid even. She was spooked and jumped at most sounds. Spending time with her and strolling in the moonlight helped her to relax—shoulders not all the way to her ears, and her voice less strained—so maybe it would just take her a little time.

"No. Just a bit uneasy about the wildlife."

Dimitri chuckled. "Good luck with that. Seriously, how are the two of you? You had your doubts about her on the show."

He was such a gossip. I stepped behind my desk to start up the computer. Hundreds of emails waited. "We're good. Everything is going as well as expected." The computer didn't want to wake. I shook my mouse.

Dimitri tapped his finger on my desk. Wrinkles had formed around his eyes. "You have been bouncing in and out of relationships lately. Maggie's a... bounce. Do not get too tied into a bounce."

Rocking back in the desk chair, I crossed my arms to face my brother-in-law, the brother of my late wife. No matter who came after his sister, my romantic life would be muddy water with Dimitri. It had been with Milly, now it was Maggie's turn. "Relationship bounces happen when you're the main lead on a dating show."

He held out his hands in a calm down motion. "I promised Irene I would take care of you. I am going to honor her wish."

I set my hands onto the cold wood of my table to grant me patience. "What do you need to say?"

"Is Maggie your midlife crisis?"

My eyes snapped to him. "No."

He stared me down and quirked up an eyebrow.

"Don't be ridiculous. Maggie and I are in a great relationship."

"What's great about it?" he fired back.

My eyes narrowed. Our relationship wasn't his business. "I like her. That's why. End of discussion." The open page on the computer finally flickered on. I typed in my password.

"No." Dimitri voice came out deep and angry.

My hands stilled on keyboard. He wasn't stopping.

"She moved to a town she doesn't love for me."

"Or for your money."

I stared at the screen for another second. My eyes flicked to my brother-in-law. "You think she's with me for my money?"

"You thought it, too."

"I never—"

"You told me so yourself."

My eyes remained on my computer screen as the screensaver perked up. "What did I say?"

"It was why you called it off with her. You said, and I quote, "I don't want to head into my twilight with dynamite no matter how much I like her."

That sounded like something I would say. Maggie told the media she wanted a place to live and land on her feet. All women were the same underneath, wanting security and money and a provider. My wife had been like that, too.

Maggie was as different from Irene as a cactus was to poppies, she didn't just want what I provided. Dimitri was wrong. She liked me and being with me, not only my money. She had pushed for time together since she arrived in Tucson, not for me to buy her things... except maybe the hot tub, though she had balked at the price, uncomfortable with me paying so much.

I pushed to my feet. Tipping forward slightly, I laid my hands on the desk and leaned across the table, toward Dimitri. "Do we have a problem?" I spoke in a low, slow voice.

We stared at each other, the man I had known for twenty years. The man who could be right with his concerns. Still, I had chosen to not entertain that doubt about Maggie. At some point, a person had to have some trust in others, or they would go bark crazy mad.

Without waiting for an answer, I sat back in my chair, smacking my keyboard to wake it up. We needed to get to work. "So, where are things with the Babbin account?"

He stepped back, still frowning. "There's a hiccup with customs, and he did not sign."

"You were supposed to secure his signature last week—"

"When you were in LA?" Dimitri fired back. "Moving Maggie?"

"Yes, when I was in LA. Moving Maggie."

"Turns out Babbin did not want to sign a contract this big with the VP. Only the CEO would do. And when the CEO couldn't be bothered to be available to sign, he got cold feet."

I rubbed my hand over my face. "He flew out here last minute. I didn't even know he was in town until I was already in LA."

"Guess he thought it's the kind of thing a president and CEO might head back into town for."

I dropped my hand.

"And he's leaving town the day after tomorrow," Dimitri concluded. "We snag him, or we lose him, and we'll be looking at letting some of the employees go since we just lost our biggest customer a few weeks ago. Get this deal, or we're talking layoffs."

"No, don't do that," I said. "I'll get him to sign, and you deal with customs?"

He held my gaze. "It's serious that we get him signed up. He was angry when you were not there."

I shrugged. "He's an uptight guy."

"Right, which is why you should have been there. Our deal is you deal with the uptight. I have never been good at it. I prefer the ones who throw their money at us."

"Do you have one of those? Because I'm in."

Dimitri didn't smile. "Are you in? Are you back? For real? Because I cannot do this without you."

"I'm in."

"What about the wedding?"

I shook my head. "Don't worry about that. That's not going to be for a long time. Work has my full focus."

"Good, then." Dimitri pressed his lips together as though to keep himself from saying anything more. "How are you going to woo Babbin back into the fold?"

"How about a barbecue and southwestern hospitality?"

He smiled a little. "Our barbecues are legend."

I smiled back. "I know."

"Barbecue and beer should work with Mr. Babbin tomorrow. Same party planner as last time?"

"Sure, whatever. Want me to call and arrange?" I asked.

He was already heading out of the room. "You'd better

if you want me to handle the customs mess so we can get back to production."

"Get cracking," I called after him.

He made a whip sound from the hallway. Things were repaired for now.

Dimitri didn't understand why I was with Maggie, and I wouldn't explain it to him. That was none of his business, despite how upset he became with his unspoken and spoken disapproval. He was being too nosey, and I had a ton of work I needed to tackle before I could reconnect with Maggie.

She didn't seem to do well being alone, and I didn't want her to stumble onto any more stuff from my previous relationships. I should have thought of that before she arrived at my house.

* * *

MAGGIE HAD PROBABLY SPENT the day unpacking and moving in. I bet she was getting tired and wanting company. I hustled to my truck, and within minutes was driving faster than I should with the window down and the wind pushing against my face, despite the heat. The intense heat made me feel alive. My skin tickled from the touch— the light scent of desert cactus flowers blooming passed by me in whiffs, easing my tense shoulder muscles.

I had forgotten about researching Mr. Babbin for tomorrow's meeting to know what angle to play. I'd do that later tonight after squeezing in time with Maggie before the sun completely sank in the sky. Maybe a bike ride up Mount Lemmon or a stroll through the oasis of

Agua Caliente Park. It sported a man-made pond that attracted hosts of birds and occasional three-foot-long tortoises.

That might be good for Maggie. Who could resist a tortoise? Once she saw this place the way I did, she'd fall in love with Tucson. The sun was lower than I had expected by the time I reached the house. We'd have to hurry if we were going to make it on an adventure before dark.

I tiptoed into the house. Sounds floated from the kitchen and, to my surprise, I found Maggie doing dishes, humming. I stepped up and wrapped my arms around her slender waist.

She wiggled underneath my touch, laughing. "You startled me."

I brushed a long strand of her blonde hair off her shoulder, my lips grazing her soft, delicate neck. Her scented perfume—a mixture of sugar and cinnamon—teased my senses. "You smell nice." I nuzzled below her ear, feeling her pulse increase, then moved from her neck to her soft lips. Our mouths gently lingered. At first, her hug was timid, which heightened my desire. There was something so charming in her innocence and shyness. She retreated from me, gasping for breath. She reached behind her back to turn off the running water. After that she wiped her hands on a dishtowel, face flushed.

"Can we talk?"

My hands dropped off her back. A spray of soap suds dripped down her cheek like my mood. Talk? In my world, when a woman asked to talk it never went well. I hadn't expected from Maggie the one question that, universally, all men hated.

I said, "Sure." But, before she could begin her spiel, I added, "But I thought we could go on a bike ride in the sunset or I'd take you to Agua Caliente Park, that has a pond and tortoises. If we don't leave right now, we'll miss it." Her teeth nibbled on her bottom lip. She avoided my eyes. This had the potential to go south. The walk or bike ride was out. I assembled my mouth into a smile and took a deep breath to soften my voice. "Okay, shoot. What is it?"

"Dee called."

I curled my hand into a tight fist. "What did she want?"

"To be my friend."

I laughed. "How'd she react when you told her to take a hike?"

"Um, well..."

My laughter stopped. "You know she's a backstabbing troublemaker who can't be trusted."

She dried her hands. "Dee asked if we had come up with the date yet."

Maggie had that panicked glint in her eyes, clearly having climbed the freight train heading toward marriage.

"We'll get there."

Maggie looked away, her neck muscles drawn tight. She didn't like hearing that.

A heaviness seeped through me. I had upset her. "Come here," I whispered, pulling her into my arms.

She leaned closely into my chest. My fingers lingered in her hair. "Do you want to get married?" Her crystal blues eyes flashed with a flicker of hope that made the pulse of my heart increase. I hurried to the kitchen table, yanked out a chair, and sat.

She was so pale and I hated seeing her upset. It made

me feel bad. But I wouldn't relent to pressure into doing a wedding too fast because it was better for a TV show schedule. That wouldn't be good for our future marriage, our relationship and, in the long run, doing what was right for us. That was what mattered. "I have work obligations that I have to do before I can think about a wedding."

Her jaw tightened as she sat. "What am I supposed to do during all that time here, not married, not committed, not sure if you'll ever commit?"

I reached over and squeezed her hand. "Find something that makes you happy..." Even as I spoke, I wondered if that would be the right answer.

"Are you putting off us getting married?"

I fingered her arm, slow small strokes. "Look, dear, I have to land this client and make sure that cell tower bounces back on its feet, or we'll have to lay off employees." I stood and moved to the kitchen sink, grabbed a glass, and filled it up with water.

"I can't do that to their families. They've been good employees." I brought her the water and set it in front of her. She sniffed before sipping her fresh water. She watched me over the rim. "You understand that, don't you?"

She wiped at the dark circles under her eyes. She looked as tired as I felt.

"I understand." She studied the kitchen table before she peered at me.

"There's a lot more to Tucson than meets the eye, Maggie. It's a kind of city that slowly reveals itself. Explore it and figure out what interests you. Meanwhile, I have an important client not happy about my absence."

She sat without moving, her face serious. "Uh, oh."

I rubbed my face. "Yeah. Uh, oh."

She settled into her seat, her face thoughtful. "Tell me about him."

I laughed. "What?"

"Your client. Tell me about him. I'm good with people. I know what paying customers want. I was the lead saleswoman in my last job."

She seemed to really be interested, and she was good with that lady last night at the hot tub store. It wouldn't hurt to give her a chance, and I needed to come up with a battle plan for tomorrow.

"He's an uptight, nervous kind of guy. He's used to having a five-star treatment and is accustomed to people being there the moment he snaps his fingers. You know the type that has too much money and expects others to serve him, not thinking that others have lives, too."

She laughed. "Oh yes, I do know the type. We had lots of those at the clothing store. What else? What does he value?"

Value? What was she getting at?

"Using a big picture lens, what's really the problem?"

I blew out a breath. "I told you."

"That was a surface excuse. Think about it, people rarely speak the real truth. Might there be something deeper going on?"

I leaned my head back, considering the question. Maggie might have a point. "I need to earn his trust or we will have to do some layoffs. If I can secure this, I don't see why we can't get married."

She was silent for a long while, apparently mulling over

the situation. "Would Austin lose his new job? He just lost his girlfriend. Remember that party at your house that one night on that trip I had here? She just took off because she didn't think Austin gave her enough attention. Austin doesn't need more bad news."

Of course, she would think of him. She was a mother—a good one, who cared about her son. Austin would be on the chopping block, especially being hired so recently. I doubted I could save him since layoffs generally started with the new hires.

"Don't think so."

"That would be horrible. I'll help. If I can," she added swiftly, her eyes uncertain. "I mean, woo-and-commit is my speed."

It was charming how much Maggie wanted to help. She was a good woman. A woman who gave up a lot to stand here by my side even though she felt completely out of place. She needed a way to fit in. I reached across the table to take her hand. "I'd love for you to be at the party tomorrow night. It'll be here. I'm hiring a catering service to barbecue for twenty to thirty business folks."

She gasped. "Oh, I'll do that. I'm much better than some company. I'll put on the home touch everyone will love."

"Will there be crepes?" I teased.

She arched a brow and pretended to be offended. "Only if you ask very nicely."

That was sweet of her to offer. It had a certain charm to it, but she didn't need to be concerned about my work. That wasn't her job. She should focus on her own stuff, not worry about me.

"But I want to help."

She didn't give up the idea quickly. "Look, dear." I leaned into her and kissed the tip of her nose. "You're tired. You're still in the midst of moving. Let's not add to your pressures."

She tilted her chin up in determination. "It wouldn't be a problem at all. I'd love to help."

"It's not a problem having the catering service do it. They do it all the time."

Her nosed wrinkled. She didn't like what I was saying.

"I'll do better than them. Guaranteed."

This seemed to matter to her and I wanted her to be happy here. Maybe I wasn't being fair and doubting her too much. She had certainly surprised me in the past. Irene liked doing it when she was around. Maybe catering was something a lot of women liked to do. Maybe it brought them joy.

"You sure?"

She beamed. "Of course."

"Then, will you do me the honor and host my company's party tomorrow?"

Maggie

My heart wouldn't stop pounding as I prepared for bed. Just thinking about JT, and the way he grinned at me when he arrived home from work caused my heartbeat to pick up speed, and my face to flush. I liked the fact we joked with each other and spent the quiet time of the evening together.

I needed to figure out the best food to prepare for the

party tomorrow. Funny, I hate cooking, and worried yesterday he would want me to do it... And today I had practically begged to not only cook for him, but thirty other people! That was insane. I shook my head. I was really going all out trying to please him, and now I would have to deliver. My stomach twisted. I have never cooked anything good before, but this time, with the plan to actually follow a recipe, I could do a good job. I hoped.

* * *

JT

The next morning my coffee maker puffed along, mixing coffee beans with water. It was almost as slow as Tucson drivers, but not quite. Ever since Maggie had complained about how slow the traffic moved when we drove into town, I noticed it more. But I'd prefer the leisurely pace to California where everyone seemed driven to hurry, then wait in long lines for most of the day and sometimes late into the evening.

My coffee pot was less than half full. I stood by the kitchen window taking in the new morning and looking for signs that Maggie was up. She had looked exhausted when we kissed goodnight.

A group of mourning doves sunned themselves in the sunrise on the telephone lines outside. I searched for the hummingbirds. They weren't out yet.

Maggie's purple shoes lay toppled over beside the couch, from when she curled into my lap last night. On the counter, she had left papers and a dirty drinking cup. Apparently, she wasn't one to pick up after herself. My house only looked this messy when the grandkids visited. I hoped this wasn't a habit of hers, to leave things everywhere. I stacked the shoes by the side door and her papers on top of them. I looked back out the window. The morning air was still and held a yellowish glow.

Movement caught my eye in the far-left corner of the yard. The closer Maggie got, the better I could see how sleepiness clung to her face. I'd never seen her anything but made up, but the tussled hair and slippers made her adorable. Soon, she reached the sliding glass door, pushed it open, and poked her head in, her eyes catching mine. "Baby?" she called out.

"Good morning. I didn't expect you up at this hour."

Confusion ran across her face. "It's after eight, and we have a menu for you to approve. Remember, you were too tired last night to plan it, and you said it was super important we got it right?"

I pecked her on her forehead. "I remember someone else who struggled to keep her eyes open."

She smiled. "I'm rested now and ready to make your party sparkle."

"Let me get more coffee, and we can dive in. Want some?"

She declined, which reminded me she was a tea person. I set a kettle of water on the stove for her.

She looked at me, hesitantly. "Want me to cook you breakfast? I don't know, maybe some sausage and eggs?"

"My stomach doesn't wake up this early."

Color returned to her face. She stepped up to me, wrapping her arms around me like she loved to do.

She smelled great. Last night's perfume still clung to

her. She rested her head on my chest. I took my coffee-free hand and placed it on the back of her head, absorbing touching her.

After a moment, she slipped to the kitchen table and pulled out her laptop and a notepad. Soon she had pulled up web pages. "Oh, I could do Niçoise crostini. Everyone loved those back home." She jotted a note down and continued to scroll.

I had no idea what she was talking about, but if it made her happy, why not.

"And I could also make grilled scallops wrapped in prosciutto."

This was starting to sound too fancy. "Sweetheart, it is Tucson. People are pretty simple here."

She waved her hand by her ear like my words were an annoying mosquito. "Once they taste it, it'll be fine. I'll also make stuffed piquillo peppers with goat cheese."

This food sounded too upscale for this crowd. These guests wouldn't appreciate it. In fact, they would make fun of it with noses turned upward. Their tastes were simpler. I stood and moved to peer over her shoulder to see what she was talking about.

She wrote again on her notepad. "I'm also going to make tamari and maple-roasted almonds, and mini Asian crab cakes with a douse of wasabi."

I looked at the pictures of these decorative foods. "Looks complicated and fancy."

Maggie beamed. "It'll be great, won't it?"

Well, she took that comment completely wrong. I walked over to the kitchen counter for another cup of coffee. It was going to be a high-volume coffee day.

Maggie's fingers continued to tap on the computer screen as she searched. "Oh, oh, oh, and a spicy raw tuna tartare on waffle chips, and for the vegetarians, Endive boats with marinated vegetables."

I leaned up against the kitchen table, seeing the screen displaying all the fancy food she was talking about. It looked like the food those elitists eat at five-hundred-dollar-a-night restaurants in uptown New York, not something people who prided themselves on being simple would want. "You do know there'll be about twenty or thirty people here tonight? That will be a lot to do in such a short time." I spoke gently, trying to guide her away from this idea.

Maggie glanced up from the computer, her large eyes taking me in. "It'll win over your client for sure. It's what your client thinks that matters, right?"

She was putting so much heart and energy into this I didn't want to burst her bubble. Maybe she was right. Maybe this would be the perfect thing and she had a secret talent for cooking that I didn't know about. I needed to give her a chance. "Right," I muttered.

She beamed. "You won't regret this."

* * *

Maggie

The pictures of the food were tantalizing. I could almost taste the explosion of flavors. I had never cooked anything like it, but it couldn't be too hard. I hoped. Unfortunately, I also needed to rush to a hairdresser. My hair hadn't taken kindly to the dry heat. It sprung into out-of-control puffy, dry curls. I scheduled an appointment at Tucson Salon of Hair then hurried to the grocery store. I couldn't find the bulb fennel for the Endive Boats or salmon roe or chervil leaves and had to resort to hunting down the store manager, a young millennial who blinked at me like I was speaking Greek. "I don't think we carry that."

Seriously, he had no clue even what I was saying. What kind of town was this? I grabbed some substitute options for the food, scallops, and a few spices and headed home certain I could still make the food taste wonderful despite the challenges.

I had no clue how to cook scallops, so I threw them in boiling water, and for the spicy raw tuna, I was short on the spices and opted for red pepper to mask the lack of other spices. By the time I was done covering the raw tuna with red, the pan with the scallops had boiled over. I YouTubed for help and continued to make a mess of things until, at last, I called the grocery store to order whatever food platters they had. "Hot spicy wings and hot peppers," they told me.

"Perfect," I half-wept into the phone, not sure if wings were good or would add to my failure.

I HUSTLED out of the hot, dry air into a blasting air-conditioned salon with hair and dirt scattered around the white tiled floor. A hairdresser with a partially shaven head, blue-green hair, and a knife tattoo on her neck looked up and greeted me. "Howdy." She was fiddling with a lady's extremely short grey hair.

All the other stylists turned to size me up. Before I could return the greeting, a young toddler with dirt smeared across his face and a glint in his eyes, jammed his walking toy straight into my legs.

"Ouch!" I yelped as the pain in my shin radiated up my leg.

I turned to leave. Coming here was clearly a mistake.

"Sit in the chair over here," the knife tattoo girl said, waving her scissors.

I'd give that more thought, but the child headed toward me for another round. I did a step ball change move to get out of his way.

The hairdresser laughed as she picked up her rugrat, and rubbed her head into his belly. He laughed an endless giggle like a stuffed doll until he was put away in his playpen. But that didn't stop this twisted nightmare. Soon, the hairdresser, Angelica, dove into working on my hair, and as she talked, she made a list of the dangers of life in the Arizonan outback.

"And of course, never, ever let a small dog or cat outside alone," she counseled firmly. *Snip, snip.*

"Oh, I know about the snakes," I replied heartily, glad to be finally certain of an answer. Also, I had JT to handle them, so...

"Nope. Hawks."

My eyes widened at my reflection in the mirror. "Hawks attack?"

"Well, they're predators, right?"

"Oh. Right," I agreed quietly.

"Everything's a predator out here." Snip, snip. Blonde wisps of my hair floated down, scattering on the floor. I pulled my gaze up and stared at her in the mirror.

"Everything?"

She nodded and lifted a length of hair between two fingers, eyeing it. "Spiders, raccoons, javelinas... Life's an earthly battle, isn't it?"

"Well, down here it is," I said tersely.

She lifted her eyes to mine in the mirror. "Just be careful of the hawks."

"And the snakes."

She smiled. "And the spiders."

"Good grief, this is the very definition of hell," I whispered.

She patted my shoulder. "Let me know if you need anything."

What had I done, coming here to the land of predators? I had moved to a town that was a setting for a horror flick. Once I walked out of the salon, my hair was flatter, but lifeless, and drooped over my eyes. My stomach twisted and my head throbbed. Maybe if I hurried, I could fix this mess of a hairstyle, but I still needed to pick up the pepper and salsa party platter. The party was set to start in fifteen minutes.

I hustled to my car and I was halfway to the grocery store when a small brown rat ran across the blacktop in front of me. I swerved to miss it, heart in my throat, not sure if dying or living upset me more.

My phone rang. Olivia, my best friend. "Save me!"

"From what?" she asked.

"There are ugly squirrels that look almost like rats or

some other disgusting creatures. The squirrel-like things have a suicidal pact to play chicken with the passing cars. It's completely insane."

"Take a deep breath," Olivia said. "Moving is always a transition." She paused before changing her voice into a cheerful tone. "I have a fan who's begging to talk with you. She needs dating advice."

I stopped short, and my newly shorn locks swung over my eye. "Me? Why?"

"Because you landed JT, I guess, in the end."

Landed. Interesting word. "That plane's still in the air," I admitted.

I pressed down harder on the pedal. Gotta grab the salsa platter and get back ASAP.

"What's wrong?" Olivia asked.

I exhaled. "Oh, nothing. Just… we haven't set a date yet."

"Uh, oh."

"No, it's fine," I said loudly. "JT has to focus on work. He has some mounting deadline. He's been so busy and… his world's pretty different than LA."

Olivia was quiet for a second. "But isn't that what you wanted? To get out of the rat race? Wasn't that your ultimate goal?"

"Ultimate," I agreed from between gritted teeth. "Tell the fan to call me. I'll do whatever I can to help."

She started to say something, but my cell reception cut out, and there was nothing left to do but grab the salsa party platter and watch out for more coyotes. I had already seen two on the way back home.

Later, the land would transform into a darkness so thick it swallowed up the sight of structures, people, and animals. The headlights of my car made a weak intrusion into the melancholy evening. The eeriness was a byproduct of a deal the city had with the university planetarium where the city didn't compete with the natural glow of stars.

The traffic light about five hundred feet ahead of me flipped to yellow. I pressed on the brakes and eased to a stop. My stomach was one dang twisted knot. I wasn't sure how any of the food was going to work out. A Chevrolet truck honked loudly behind me. I jumped. My eyes flashed to the dashboard. I needed to greet the guests in less than ten minutes. A growing pressure filled my chest.

The night was black. Muggy. I drove faster than I should, but I had to arrive to the party to be the star, the gracious one, the hostess, JT's perfect match. I had promised him I could pull this off. I had to prove it. Plus, win over the potential client. If I could do that, JT would see that I fit in.

I hadn't entered into his world as strong as I dreamed, but I hadn't realized the ruggedness of this place… town… city. I hadn't understood the hardiness of the setting. Never would I have imagined so many animals running wild. A place with almost a million people, counting the outlying area, and it acted like a freckin' outdoor zoo. Impossible to prepare for that. None of the Internet sites had posted a warning about that. The littering of potholes, yes, but not the even more disturbing reality of all the wildlife and its predator mentality.

But the point was I could help JT, if I arrived on time, and did my razzle dazzle show. I knew I could. Hoped I could…

A chill shot down my arms and neck as I pressed the accelerator. I was late. Guests must have already arrived. I hadn't gotten the kitchen cleaned properly. I hadn't changed into my fancy dress clothes, and my hair was a limp mess. I flicked at my bangs, looked into the rearview mirror, and pressed hard on the gas pedal as the yellow headlights disturbed the black cloak of the evening.

CHAPTER 6

*M*aggie

A HUGE WALL of longing for the ocean, green grass, culture, and people who knew how to drive fast swelled and crashed inside my chest as I pulled into JT's dirt driveway. I bumped up the long path, pebble rocks crunching from the pressure of the tires. Tension squeezed at my throat as I rolled up to the house and saw the guests had beat me here.

Chevy trucks—lots of those—and a Ford truck with a gun rack in the window were parked every direction, including in front of the garage. I squinted to see if a gun hung on the rack, but I couldn't tell. Almost all the cars were coated in dust. This sight would be unheard of in LA —the lack of order, the overabundance of trucks, the dirt.

It wouldn't be dusty in LA, I thought, carefully navigating my way between a Chevy pick-up and a motor-cycle to the back of the house. Of course, half of these people wouldn't even be here yet if we were in LA. The traffic was always brutal, no matter the day or time.

Score one for Nowheresville.

Shadows and light flickered inside the house. I peered into the rearview mirror and ran my fingers over stray strands of hair, then stopped and stared at the figure coming out of the back door, tumbling down the steps, just like... just like...

"Austin!" I cried and flung the door open. "Baby, when did you get here?"

Austin was twenty-one years old, red haired, and a slender toothpick, who hated when I call him baby. But I'd been calling my only child "baby" since the moment they laid him in my arms. I wasn't going to stop now, no matter how hard he rolled his eyes. He circled to the back of the car, gesturing.

"Open the hatch, Mom," he called.

"Open the hatch?" I echoed, climbing out of the car. "Come here and give your mom a hug. When did you get here? Why are you here?"

He did a U-turn and came back to give me a hug. I threw my arms up around his shoulders and held him a second longer.

"JT asked me to stop by."

"That was nice of him," I muttered, not sure if that showed doubt on JT's part or if he was being thoughtful.

"It's your first shindig out here. He thought it might be good to have me here."

"Aw," I said again, then hesitated and gave that some thought. "Why?"

He patted me on my shoulder and hurried back to the trunk. "He thought you might need help. Open the hatch."

"He thought I'd need help?" I repeated, reaching for my keys to click the button. The hatch beaped and slowly rose. Austin's head disappeared into the car as a tiny lingering doubt lodged in my stomach. I went up to help Austin with the bags, hoping this didn't mean JT thought I'd be as much of a misfit at his party as I *knew* I'd be. Was Austin here to arm me with some familiar support?

"Mom," he said under my strain, "You need to get in there. JT keeps asking for you, and so do the other guests."

I let my arms fall to my side. "Oh, yeah. Right."

I saw the strain around Austin's eyes. He had recently lost a girl he was completely enamored with to another guy. It had torn him to shreds to the point he was unwilling to even look at another girl or talk about it. I could still hear the strain and the sadness of it in his voice. The last thing I wanted was to add to that sadness. I grabbed two bags. "Okay, let's go conquer the get-together."

He didn't laugh. Instead, he glanced at the house then lowered his voice. "Mom, I wanted to warn you. The food you put out…"

I froze, grocery bags dangling from my hands. I glanced at the lighted windows. The sound of laughter trickled out onto the veranda. "What?"

"It was…"

Too spicy? Too LA? Too much dairy? The options whirled through my head.

"Awful."

My jaw dropped. "What?"

"It looks funny, and it tastes weird."

"I—no, I… It can't be weird. I followed the recipes." I looked at the dark silhouette of JT's house and the lights spilling down the stairs, the happy people inside laughing… *at my food?*

My breath became shallow. "I followed the recipes," I repeated.

Austin sighed. "Yeah, but Mom, you suck as a cook."

I whirled on him. "But I tried—"

"But why? You have always been bad. You never follow any instructions. You feel too constricted being told what to do with all those recipe directions."

I stopped short at his comment. "But this time I followed them as best as I could," I whispered.

We stared at each other in the incandescent light spilling down the back stairs.

"Why did you even bother trying?" Austin asked quietly, "When you know you're not good at all, and you don't even want to be good at it? You hate cooking. You have always hated it."

I blinked. "Well, because JT asked—"

"He said you offered to do the food. That you wanted to. That you insisted."

"Well, I thought I could do it by actually following the recipe."

I wanted to contribute to his life, his business. I wanted to make JT happy and be the perfect wife. But Austin was right, I hated cooking and never once did a good job at it. But JT wanted a wife who cooked well, and since I was going to be his wife, that meant I cooked good food…

and... oh, dammit. It was all very confusing, and I had apparently really messed up.

The crispiness of the evening tickled me with chills. "Okay, tell me the truth: how bad is it?" I asked.

He grimaced. "The shrimp was... inedible."

I groaned. He gave me a gentle shoulder bump. The plastic bags in our arms swayed. "Stop trying to be someone you're not, Mom. You're fine the way you are."

I stared at the house, not sure if I was ready for this.

He nudged me. "You can charm your way out of anything, even bad food."

I tugged down my dress. "You're right. At least I have freckin' hot wings and peppers, dip, and salsa."

"Yuck." Austin stuck out his tongue.

"Party favorites."

"But jalapeno peppers?" Austin asked.

We'd come to a foreign land.

The back door swung open. JT stood there, a silhouette of a masculinity staring out at us.

"Austin, good work." He smiled before swinging his gaze to me. "Hi, sweetheart." He swept the party trays out of my hand. In one grand gesture, he jostled most the grocery bags off my arm.

"There was a lady with a knife tattoo at the hair salon." I fluffed my hair as we hurried into the kitchen.

He looked over his shoulder, startled. "Your hair looks nice."

My heart skipped a beat, glad he liked it. "Thanks." Maybe he wasn't as upset with me for being late as I supposed, but that didn't stop my pressing need to continue explaining. "And a squirrel was in the road. And did you know hawks are predators?"

He chuckled. "Yes, they are." He slid the trays onto the counter and took my hand. "Ready to meet everyone?"

I pasted a smile on my face. "Am I ever!"

"The guests have been anxious to meet you."

My legs weakened. I tugged at my bangs to brush them to the side of my face. The loose strand of hair fell back into my eyes.

Finding my strength, I looked at him, "Sorry. Things got crazy." I let that settle as a door banged in the distance from Austin heading in. "I really messed this up." My voice cracked, fighting tears. I shuffled the grocery bags in my arms, peering down into the darkness.

JT reached out and tenderly wiped at a stray tear. "Sweetheart, don't worry about it."

I sniffed, trying to get a grip.

"You're here, and that's all that matters."

I wiped at my face to erase traces of any other spare tear. "Austin said that everyone already hates my food."

JT pressed down on my shoulder. "Never let them see you rattled. March in there, head held high like you own the place like you did when we first met. That was attractive."

I flashed a smile at him. "You liked that?"

He quirked an eyebrow. "Yep. You stood out like you knew you were the only one for me."

I batted my eyes. "I *was* the only one for you."

He laughed. "That's very true." He seized my hand and pulled me to him. "Round two to show your confidence."

I squeezed his large, strong hand, ready to be his super-confident sidekick. "Is the big dog client here, yet?"

JT peered toward the road. He shifted his weight like he was pumping himself up for the big game. "Not yet."

Relief washed through me. I had time to turn around the crowd before Mr. Future showed up.

The rumbling noise of the guests invited us to join in. "I'm armed with jalapeño peppers."

"What?" JT opened the door for me to go through into the kitchen.

He plopped the stuff he was carrying on the counter and focused on me. "The most helpful thing you can do right now is make sure everyone feels welcome in such a way they forget the food."

I looked over the table to assess Austin's judgement of the condition of the food. "I'm staying here until the food is satisfactory."

Austin, standing by the sink, piped up, "I threw out the shrimp since there was speculation about food poisoning."

"Food poisoning?" I whispered.

The stuffed piquillo peppers with goat cheese sat there, apparently untouched, so was my attempt at roasted almonds, and marinated vegetables that had gone soggy.

JT strolled over to the food, eyes narrowing as he assessed the display in a business-like fashion. It was clear that pleasing him wasn't a sure thing. My fingers fidgeted. I fumbled, pulling out the fruit and veggie trays and, of course, the magic weapon—wings and peppers. He picked up a stuffed piquillo pepper and popped it into his mouth. "This is good." He pointed to the pepper.

Austin broke into our conversation. "Mom, forks? Napkins?"

I turned to my boy. "Did you not hear what JT just said? He said the peppers were good. Good. I bought good peppers. He actually said it!"

Austin rolled his eyes. "Okay, Mom. You won that round."

JT rested his hip against the table and swung a look between Austin and me. "You worried your food isn't good?"

"Austin said it was awful, but don't worry, I know how to save a show. I have backup." I gestured to the bags. "Wings. Peppers. Salsa. Local favorites… and you liked it."

He glanced at the bags and pushed them off to the side.

I touched him lightly on the forearm, resisting playing with his thick dark arm hair. "I'll handle the food. You go entertain your guests. I'll join you once this is fixed."

He nodded, knowing that was what he should do. But he added, "Never let them see you're scared. They can smell fear. You must convey confidence."

"You make it sound simple."

He gave me a slow smile. "You know how many deals I've worked? How many times I thought it was all over, and then lost the deal?"

"Never?" I guessed.

He laughed and reached for my hand. "Happens all the time. But the art of the deal is confidence. Never back down, never back up. Everything's a show. Present what you've got like there's no way they could say no, and they'll say yes."

I wasn't sure that applied to shrimp scampi, but JT did

know about wheeling and dealing. After one last look at the bags of food, I weaved my fingers with his and nodded.

"Okay, then. The food's great, and we all love it."

"Mom, where're the forks and napkins?"

I stared at my boy. What was he asking?

"Where are the forks? You know the stuff people eat food with."

Forks. Napkins… crap. I had forgotten them.

"And the avocados? I don't see any of them. I thought you were going to make dip? Everyone's asking for it."

Before I could answer, a big pack of women strolled into the room. "JT!" They gathered around him, more enthusiastic than a swarm of mosquitoes.

"Hello, ladies," he said with a smile and more warmth and excitement than I thought necessary. "Let me introduce my fiancée, Maggie."

A round of unfelt "hi's" and "hello's" flittered through the group, despite the fact the women were either eyeing JT or the food.

I opened the veggie tray, scooted it to the center of the wooden table, plus the peppers, and made sure that seasoned cream cheese was right next to it. "Wings, salsa, and peppers," I called like I had struck a cattle bell announcing dinner on a farm.

That drew a few women from JT to the table. I circled around the guests as they picked up a paper plate. I hustled my high heels, tapping loudly on the cement floor, as I made my way to JT's side. Several women glanced at my feet with a curled nose.

Self-conscious, I looked down. My dark purple pedicure was in decent shape with only a few chips here and there, but no condition to allot the disdain. Curious, I scoped out the room to note I was the only one in heels. I didn't even see a two-inch or one-inch heel, just a lot of open toed shoes, mostly sandals. Blue was a popular color, and so was pink, no purple of any shade. How did they avoid cactus claws with flat sandals?

Apparently, I was the only one who embraced the joy of deep purple as well as being the only one with a diamond stud on the big toe to add a pop. My sparkly toes stood out, but not in a good way.

JT's gaze swung my direction. He smiled at me. I closed my eyes to soak it in. Maybe everything would be okay, after all. Feeling his encouragement, I extended my hand out to the first lady who stood in front of me. "Hi, I'm Maggie."

My first victim wore a summer tank top and cropped pants, no makeup, short grey hair going every which way. She scanned me up and down, lips pursed. My tight blue and red party dress with sparkles suddenly seemed too much. This woman still hadn't shaken my hand. I let my arm slip to my side, hoping no one noticed. Growing warm, I rambled, "It was sure hot out today, wasn't it?"

She blinked. "It always is in the summer."

I sighed and tried my second attempt at small talk. "I'm new here, and I have no idea how you guys survive it."

She raised her water bottle that I hadn't noticed her holding. "We prepare." She had no ring on the ring finger but plenty of attitude.

I brushed my hair onto the back of my shoulder. "That makes sense."

"Where are you from?"

That question thankfully came from a younger party-goer in a breezy summer dress, with light pearls circling her neck. She had makeup on and was quite pretty with long dark curls, and a welcoming demeanor with sweet, mid-western features.

"Sunny, Southern California." I beamed, glad to finally land on a comfortable topic. But from the expressions that raced through the group, it wasn't cool to be from California.

"I brought more food and refreshments," I said like an informative host. "We have salsa, and jalapeño peppers, which is supposed to be a crowd favorite, and several white and red wines."

"Wine is better," someone muttered.

"That other stuff you had out was disgusting," came a whisper.

"Where?" came a louder voice from a lady across the room—her hair short, face pinched, and food on her mind.

"Kitchen table," I spoke in a pleasant tone. Although I was finding the confidence act hard, I forced a smile. Only a few more hours with these people, then it would be over. That might be doable.

My eyes found JT, and he winked at me.

I winked back. I squared my shoulders. "I want everyone to know I'm going to take good care of JT. Last night we picked out a hot tub for him to slip into at night when he gets home all achy and tired from working."

Women literally shook their heads in front of me, and one said loud enough so everyone could hear it, "What a gold digger."

JT must have sensed the hostility of the crowd. He

crossed the room quickly to stand by my side. "Everything going okay?" he asked. He took my hands into his.

People shifted weight, cleared throats, and coughed.

"I was telling them about our new hot tub."

He nodded. "Looking forward to it." He squeezed my fingers before greeting more incoming guests and steering them outside.

A deejay and his people brushed past me, carrying equipment, and instruments to set up for the live entertainment. Anything I said to these people seemed wrong. I headed to the kitchen and grabbed a glass of water. I could still hear the ladies, and a man here and there, talk about hikes they took up Sabino Canyon over the weekend. The waterfall was full this year and, apparently, they saw several bobcats and a rattler. That knowledge didn't make my stomach feel any better.

I couldn't listen to any more of this. I stepped outside and was greeted by a perfect evening, the temperature in the low nineties, which felt surprisingly pleasant after being in triple digits all day. I looked up to see a few stars popping out to say hi. Even out here, the laughter and talking was at a low roar. Judging from the noise, the liveliest part of the party was in the farthest corner of the yard by the big Velvet Mesquite tree. I saw JT drinking a glass of wine there.

I hurried to the kitchen to grab a bottle of Sonoma Valley red wine and a few glasses, then back outside. Wine had to be the best way to the hearts of these Tucsonans.

I wandered from group to group, offering, "Wine?"

A few agreed and thanked me, but conversations full of luster slipped into silence the moment I stepped up. After the third time, I hesitated before going up, finding it harder to find my smile. I was a confident person, but this crowd was brutal. Maybe the harsh land made them harsh people.

One of the ladies in the next group took a sip of the wine. "What is this?"

I perked up. Maybe I found someone, at last, I could talk to. "It's from Northern California in the Sonoma Valley. This wine is all the rage there. Everyone loves its soft subtle undertones."

The lady pursed her lips and said, "Oh," before putting her wine glass down on the table behind her.

Anger flared in my chest. "Do you have something against California?"

She squared her jaw as I looked down on her since she was at least a half foot smaller than me and wore no heels. "In fact, I do. We have all you Californians flooding our town." She tipped her chin up. "You go on and on about how great California is and how it's the best. We wish you'd just keep your attitude and opinions back where they belong: California. We're simple here. We don't need all those airs."

It'd be so easy to rip into this holier-than-thou woman, but I flicked a look over at JT, who nodded at some businessperson. I better not. My grip tightened on the wine bottle.

"It's a good thing I am not one of those," I said lightly. I turned to a guest behind me. "Wine?"

After pouring a glass for a woman who smiled at the California-hater and nodded at me, I gravitated to the group with JT.

"And that's when I decided the company was never

going to be worth what they asked us to invest, so we pulled out."

A tall, red-faced man in a cowboy hat gave an incredulous guffaw. "JT, that company was worth over a million dollars."

JT smiled. "And how much is it worth now?"

The red-faced man shrugged. "Not sure. Haven't heard much about them lately…"

"Exactly. They folded, about six months ago. They were entrepreneurs, which is great until it's not. Those guys couldn't handle that company long-term, and they weren't interested in feedback on how to improve. They were flash, not substance. Not the sort of company to sink a lifetime's worth of money into."

Everyone nodded and started sharing their own stories of poorly run companies they'd worked with. I shivered—I didn't know why—as I drew up behind JT.

His dark eyes swung to me, and the edge of his mouth curved upwards.

"Hi," I said softly.

He tugged me into the circle, right by his side. A shiver raced down my back just by standing by his side where I belonged.

"Who is this beautiful young lady?" asked a curly white-haired man with weathered skin.

JT nudged me closer. "This is my fiancée, Maggie."

He shook my hand. "Are you sure you want to be with this character?"

"We'll see," I said.

He laughed. "Whoo-hoo. You got a spitfire here."

JT squeezed my shoulders closer to him. "That I do."

Before I could say anything to JT, my phone buzzed. Not wanted to be rude, I excused myself and moved from the center of the crowd to answer it a few feet away. I strained to hear but couldn't decipher the faint voice over the noise of the party.

I nodded at JT then moved farther away from the noise of the crowd.

"I can't believe I'm talking to you..." It took more gushing before I realized this must be the fan Olivia told me about. "It's so wonderful how you won at the end."

Won. I looked at JT. I failed this party. I failed to have a marriage date. I failed getting along with the locals. I should worry that at some point, JT would conclude I didn't belong in his life.

"I just can't believe I'm talking to you," continued the phone caller. "My name is Zianne, and I just know you can help me because you had completely lost, you had all the other girls against you, you had JT against you... Now look at you. You're on top of it all."

"How can I help you?" I asked to get her to stop rambling about all my failures.

"I don't know how to get a guy." The desperateness in her voice was palpable. "You seem to be able to attract them in the midst of a ton of beautiful girls. That's a talent."

"Attracting and keeping men are two different things. Let me tell you."

She stopped talking. I could feel her listening hard. Fine. I would tell her what I knew.

"It's about how you make the man feel. They need to feel comfortable around you and see that you fit in their life. Men love women they fit with. If a man likes high maintenance, a show piece, it's fine to be high mainte-nance. But if he doesn't, you have to dial it back."

JT didn't like high maintenance.

"So, kind of follow his lead?" Zianne asked.

"Become part of his world..." I struggled to come up with words to explain what it was that I did. Even as I said it, something felt off. I didn't know why—it was as accu-rate a description as any other.

I'd grown up watching people. I especially liked watching healthy couples—the couples who actually liked being together and held hands years after the newness had worn off. I watched how the women were. They made their man comfortable. They made sure he had a place in her life. The woman looked at him with loving tenderness and, in return, the man worshipped her. He would do anything for her, including opening doors and not noticing any other woman in the room. A man needed to know he was safe and fit into the woman's world. I could be a fire-cracker, but I knew how to turn it off, most of the time. I knew how to help him feel attracted to me. I knew how to keep myself safe in this game.

"Ahhh," Zianne whispered, "I think I get it."

I barely heard the rest of her reply as I eyed several women in a semi-circle around JT, like he was a rock star. Several times, one of them would reach out and touch his forearm or give her hair a subtle flip.

The women were certainly attracted to something. I wasn't sure if it was his confidence, as he claimed, or his power as a boss, or the fact he was damn good-looking. Women were suckers for all of the above, and they weren't afraid to show their attraction.

Keep your hands off my man. I drew in a shaky breath. I would have to get used to this crap.

"So, I have to do whatever possible for them to feel at home?"

Zianne's words snapped my attention to the phone. I turned away from JT and the circle of his admirers. "Yes, you got it," I said firmly. "Whatever it takes."

Whatever it takes.

It was time to hurry this conversation along. I needed to find JT's new clients. "Was that helpful?" I asked.

"A lot. I am going to bring cookies to my guy at work. He loves a girl who cooks. I don't really like cooking, but I'm sure it'll be fine…"

I felt the dragging sensation again.

"You're so awesome. I always voted for you. I'm going to tell all my friends how cool you are. They're going to have to eat crow."

I blinked.

"How much do I owe you?"

That was awkward. "Go attract Mr. Wonderful," I said. "I'll count that as payment. Happy attraction."

I went back inside, slid my phone under a bowl of bananas in the kitchen, and hurried to find Mr. Babbin before the evening got too late.

CHAPTER 7

$\mathcal{M}$aggie

CLOUDS PASSED OVER THE MOON, making the night darker. JT still leaned toward the ladies engulfed in conversation, with no sign of his important guest. Austin strolled up to me with dirty wine glasses in his hand that he had collected. "Mom, how's it going?"

I shrugged then thought better of it. I could talk to my boy. He understood me better than any other living soul. "You know, not sure how to fit into this world."

"Do you need to?" The glasses he held clinked against each other. "You have been a free bird ever since I've known you. You never conformed well."

I peered over at JT, who was now laughing at something someone said. His rough good looks were apparent even across the yard. That man could steal my breath without even trying. I loved that. "But if JT doesn't see me fitting in his world, it might not work."

"Why are you worried about that?" Austin asked as though I was being stupid.

JT must have felt my eyes on him. He looked over to us and gave me a smile and a nod. I waved back to him, lightly flushing.

To Austin, I said, "Because we are new and still figuring things out."

My boy shrugged. "I don't know anything about that. But what I can tell you is JT doesn't like messes, and the kitchen looks like something exploded in it."

I stared at my boy. Was JT a clean freak? I had thought his house was super clean because of the maids, and he was the only one living there. The grandkids did visit often, and there was no sign of that. His garage had been extremely organized, especially for a garage. Maybe he was. There was so much to learn about the man, and if he did care about things being clean, I should hurry and clean the kitchen. Then, when he arrived, charm Mr. Babbin. Forget getting along with the women for now, since it wasn't working anyway.

Another cloud moved off the moon, spilling more light on my path, guiding my boy and me back to the kitchen. No sooner had Austin and I started working on the dishes than we heard someone outside of the house near the sliding door.

"Can you believe that Maggie? She's acting like she is too good for us with all that California and hot tub talk. She certainly isn't. What a gold digger."

Damn.

"Mom, don't listen."

I waved my hand by my ear to hush Austin up. I most definitely wanted to hear what these frontier women had to say. I wanted to know what I was up against.

"She thinks she's something special."

More like, right for JT. Not necessarily special.

"Can you believe the food? Like anyone would even consider eating that crap."

Snickers.

"My ten-year-old could have done a better job."

Austin rolled his eyes and shook his head. Probably his effort to lessen the sting of their comments, sweet boy.

The women continued, "I don't think anyone touched it before her son threw it out."

"I wonder what JT was thinking," came a high-pitched voice. "He could have had anyone, and he chose… her."

"A spoiled, gold digger, city girl."

Austin put his hand on my shoulder. I shook it off.

"She couldn't be more different from Irene."

"Did you see how she begged everyone to drink more. Irene would never have done that. She was too refined."

"I can't see JT staying with her."

My heart beat hard in my ears, blocking their words. I couldn't hear the next few lines, but I did decipher the word "show," along with the deep understanding that I wasn't the most popular girl in town.

Having a mother who liked to drink a bottle as much as mine did in public meant mean girls were nothing new. My mom drank like a fish. In public. *Very* public. Like in the town commons. The bank. In church a couple of times a year. It didn't make me very popular with the other kids or their parents.

"Heard your mom was stumbling around drunk last night," they'd sneer, as if they didn't already know.

"Stay away from that one. The apple doesn't fall too far from the tree." As if I was already condemned to be like my mom for just being born to her.

The worst time was at the prom when I was with Charlie, my boyfriend at the time. My mom, who had volunteered to supervise, had stumbled into the dance floor, confused, bumbling, and flirting with Charlie. She had even grabbed his backside before throwing up in the middle of the dance floor. The school photographer had captured the event for all to remember.

Those pictures made the rounds with quiet chuckling and glances in my direction. I was the child of the parent who had stunk up prom night. No other teenager could relate. I was the odd one who, no matter what I said or did, wouldn't quite fit. Kind of like now.

Enough of that. I wouldn't stand by watching people scoff at me and have that disdain spread like a disease like it had to my boyfriend. I hadn't done anything to stop it then, but now that I was an adult, I most certainly would fight the damage of idle whispers. I strolled over to the sliding glass door and popped the porch lights on and off several times before leaving them on. Loud gasps erupted from the gossiping gals. "Who turned those on?"

"It's probably her."

"Do you think she heard us?"

"She had to."

A long "shh!" sounded, followed by quick footsteps

walking away. Hopefully, the light switch would kindle a low-grade worry in their souls that others might be listening to their meanness.

Austin stared at me, soap suds up to elbows. "That was certainly one way to handle that."

I wiggled my eyebrows. "I still have some tricks."

The dishes could wait. Reminding JT why he picked me, couldn't. "I am going to freshen up and get back out there."

"Mom, I'm leaving after I finish the dishes."

That took me by surprise but, of course, he would want to leave. He was young and had other things he wanted to do.

"Okay, baby." I stepped up to him, standing on my tippy toes to kiss him. "Thank you for your support."

After our goodbyes, I dashed into JT's back bathroom to double-check my hair. Satisfied, and heading out the bedroom door, I spotted a clear vase on top of the chest of drawers. Sticks poked out of it with folded colored papers attached. Standing on my tippy-toes, I reached for the decoration and pulled the vase down to see what it was. I put the vase on the counter, picked up one of the pieces of paper, and unfolded it. I read in a girl's handwriting, *"I love how you take care of me."* A knot formed in my stomach. *"I love how you smile and cook such great food."*

I stared at the feminine handwriting, working out that these were love notes from his wife to JT. This house was becoming a museum of all of JT's former lovers—female products and bare walls and love notes.

The paper shook in my hands.

He'd said the same thing to me in a note once. Pink

paper with blue violets on it. *Where did he get this?* I'd wondered at the time. His confident scrawl covered the page with a few short, powerful words, *"I like how you took care of me on the show."*

Well, now I knew where he'd gotten the paper from. His wife's stationery.

I forced my breath to slow. It wasn't unusual for a guy to use the same gestures with each woman he created a relationship with. That was to be expected. I guess. I couldn't help but to want to be different. Special. I didn't want to be a replacement of his wife but, apparently, if I was going to be a replacement, I'd have to learn how to actually cook. That might be a deal breaker for JT. Hopefully, getting along with all his guests wasn't a deal breaker.

I put the paper back into the vase. Competing with the dead was becoming an impossible fight. If I tossed these notes out, like I had the cookbooks, it would be pushing it too far. I carefully put the vase back where I found it.

My chest tightened. These notes were more personal than a cookbook, and from his dead wife. He had kept the notes here even during Milly's stay, and hadn't thought to remove them when he knew I was coming. I closed my eyes to find the strength to climb back into my high heels. They made my legs look great…

I slipped them on, then moved to the big window. People milled around the back deck. I spied JT's Mr. Babbin. It had to be him from the way he held himself and the shiny suit he wore. His girlfriend stood with him under a string of lights. She was dressed to the nines, in heels higher than mine and makeup that must have taken an hour to apply. She looked bored.

Babbin was talking earnestly to her. Still bored.

She glanced at her phone and dropped it back into her purse, making a gesture toward the house. Mr. Babbin scowled then he threw out his arms in a gesture of defeat. She signaled for them to go inside.

She wanted to leave.

Again, I understood that feeling. I wished I'd run into her earlier. We probably could have had a nice conversation about how bored we were.

Babbin pulled out his car keys.

I stiffened. He was leaving?

If Babbin was going to walk out the door, JT was going to lose this account. I glanced at her again and had an idea. Before I could think about it too hard, I strode outside, past the mean girls—ignoring them entirely—and headed directly to Mr. Babbin. Or, rather, his girlfriend.

JT was still the center of the party. He was a light to bugs in a black night. Everyone was magnetically pulled to him, and I guess I was one of those people, too.

"Welcome," I held my hand out to the girlfriend.

She shook it. "Thanks," she muttered.

Relief clearly flushed through Mr. Babbin's face. "Finally, someone who knows how to dress for a party." He saluted me with his glass of wine.

I laughed. "I'm learning it's a little more upscale than the way they do things around here."

"You aren't from around here, are you?"

I laughed. The first time tonight, it seemed like it was okay to be different. "How can you tell besides my dress and heels?"

He smiled. "Well…" He looked me over, as his beautiful

lady with olive skin, a firm jawline, and a sleek black dress hooked his elbow. "The locals have a certain look." He glanced to his girlfriend, tightening his elbow against his side to tuck her hand closer. "This is my girlfriend, Rebecca. And you are?" he asked, turning back to me.

I beamed, "Maggie." I found the courage and held out my hand to the woman. "Nice to meet you."

She shook my hand with a long, firm grip. "You, too." She leaned into me and whispered, "So, what is there to do here for sanity?"

Even though there wasn't anyone around our corner of the party, I lowered my voice to a deep whisper, "I have no idea. I just arrived here yesterday."

Rebecca laughed. "You're finding it hard here, too?"

"Yes!" I exclaimed. I had just stumbled onto my new best friend.

The man tapped her on her shoulder. "Dear, I'm going to go do some business."

She nodded, not taking her focus from our conversation. "It's so damn hot here!"

I leaned toward her and said in full agreement, "Hotter than hell."

She smiled. "Ain't it the truth? And the women here are pieces of work."

I burst into laughter. I couldn't have said it more perfectly if I tried. "I'm glad I'm not the only one who is having a hard time here."

"You would have to be crazy, not to."

My swollen feet pressed into the straps of my shoes. "Up for wine straight from the California vineyards?"

We took our conversation, insults, and sarcasm into the house.

* * *

JT

As Mrs. Miller rattled on about her desert garden and the wildlife it attracted, I searched over the crowd to see Maggie. I couldn't keep my thoughts off of the most alluring woman at the party as I chatted with my guests. Maggie looked rattled when she arrived, with deep worry lines on her face, breathing heavy, and flustered. I didn't care she had made a mess of the food, but that didn't seem to stop her from worrying about it.

For a while she moved across the lawn, going from group to group offering wine. She wasn't smiling, and a couple of times, I watched her wobbling in her shoes like the cactus injury still bothered her. I hadn't seen her like this before—lips drawn tight and shoulders pulled up to her ears.

I shouldn't have tied the wedding date to the result of a business deal. I'd been doing business deals for decades. I could do them in my sleep. Deals were my comfort zone: I was great at them. But deals didn't mesh well with home life. From now on, I'd keep business and Maggie separate.

As I continued to entertain, I lost sight of Maggie. With the wine flowing, the wealthy visitors and friends hadn't grown bored of exchanging war stories. Finally, after what seemed like hours, I spotted Mr. Babbin.

I excused myself from the group to greet him. "Good to see you. Glass of wine? Food?"

He patted his stomach. "Had too much already. I'm on the clock, so let's get down to business. I have a few questions about operations."

We dove into the nitty gritty details, but Mr. Babbin kept glancing away like he was worried about something else. After I answered a number of his questions, he cleared his throat and excused himself.

I took the time to look for Maggie. I needed to see her. I needed to know she was happy and not just filling wine glasses. To my surprise, after a few minutes of me wandering and managing short conversations with guests, Mr. Babbin jogged up to my side. Apparently both Rebecca and Maggie were missing.

He shook his head as we stepped up onto the back patio. "She's against living here to do this project, and tells me this town is dreadful."

I nodded, giving myself time to digest the bad news. "Maybe we should take her and Maggie to Old Town Tucson. That might change her mind."

"Doubt that," Mr. Babbin said. "I could hardly keep her at the party to talk to you."

I gestured toward the door. "Maybe they're in the house."

We headed inside as Mr. Babbin talked. "I need her to be pleased or this isn't going to work. I have to put her first. I hope you understand." His voice held the committed, flat, tone hardened businessmen take on when their minds are made up and they want no more argument. "These women of ours, JT, they need more than...this." He swept his arm around, indicating the desert landscape. "Nope, I can't do this to my lady. I can't bring her here."

I swallowed a lump in my throat, dreading telling Dimitri. Despite Mr. Babbin's tone, I pushed on anyway. "Are you sure there isn't anything we can do to change your mind? We'd really like to have your business and will do a spectacular job for you."

He gave my words a nod like he was considering it. "We'll keep you in mind." He slapped me on the shoulder. "I am sure you understand keeping the woman happy."

My vision narrowed as I looked at him. My throat constricted. Overcoming romantic relationship issues was almost impossible. My fingers started twitching on my pant leg as I thought of what would happen to the employees and their families if I didn't make this happen. There had to be some way to turn this around. I slid open the screen door to the house. Once inside, Maggie's and Rebecca's voices stopped us. They were in the living room around the corner, talking.

"How are we supposed to live with them?" Rebecca asked.

Maggie laughed. "It's a challenge."

Mr. Babbin and I exchanged eye contact, but stayed silent, lurking.

Maggie went on. "I have to admit, while I'm frustrated with some of the things he does, I have to remind myself, one of the greatest things about JT is he's stable. Super reliable."

Rebecca made a sound. Agreeing? Harrumphing?

Babbin and I exchanged glances again.

"All sorts of crazy things happened on the show," Maggie continued. "But he took everything in stride whether there was a camera around or not. He's steady and does what he says. He's exactly what he appears."

I shifted weight on my feet, my face flushing.

"Oh-h, that's really important," Rebecca said.

"It is. Reliable and steady are seriously underrated."

After a moment of quiet, Rebecca said in a quiet voice, "You know what, thank you. You're right, Kevin's strongest trait is his reliability, and I… I might have been forgetting how much it matters. I mean, I've been with some guys who…"

Her voice drifted off. Babbin and I unconsciously leaned closer.

Maggie laughed. "Oh, I get it. Guys who promise one thing, but the moment something better comes along, they're out. Guys who are all sparkle but no substance. I know that guy, too."

Rebecca, after another moment of silence, made a frustrated noise. "You know, I've been mad at Kevin all day. He can be frustrating and stubborn, and he dragged me out here to this place where it's hotter than a roaster."

"But he dragged you," Maggie said softly.

Confusion deepened Rebecca's voice. "Right, I know, that's what I just said."

"No." I heard a wine glass set on the table. "I'm saying he dragged *you*. You. He brought you with him here because…"

"Because… he promised me he'd take me on his next business trip."

"So, he came through for you."

"Yeah." Rebecca's voice was reflective now. "He came through."

"And you haven't been too much fun on this trip?"

Rebecca laughed. "I haven't been at peak performance, no. I warned him, though."

"And he still brought you."

Silence radiated.

Maggie spoke again. "I know you said you weren't getting along, but it's obvious he really cares about you. That man looks at you with so much love in his eyes."

"He does?"

Mr. Babbin and I both shrugged, not sure what to do about the fact that we were eavesdropping. But we couldn't interrupt them now, they'd know we heard them.

"He got the two of us talking, too."

Rebecca sighed. "He did do that. Hey, Maggie."

"Yeah?"

"If you're living here in town. I don't know, maybe… maybe I could handle it here, after all."

Mr. Babbin cleared his throat quietly and turned to me. "Let's meet tomorrow morning. But, right now, I need to get my lady home."

I nodded as he moved into the room to collect Rebecca, and they said their goodbyes. As soon as they moved out of view, I walked over close to Maggie, who was picking up wine glasses.

"Put those down for now," I whispered in her ear.

She turned toward me. "What's so important for me to stop cleaning?"

My hand slipped down into hers. "Trust me."

I guided her out onto the porch to the remaining party-goers. I cleared my throat as everyone gathered around. "I have an announcement to make," I said.

The party hushed and everyone stared at me. "I want you all, my close friends and colleagues, to know that we..." I gestured to Maggie at my side, "will be getting married at the end of the month."

During their weak applause, Maggie threw her arms around me in a tearful squealing hug. "We're setting a date!"

I smiled. "Yes, baby. We are."

CHAPTER 8

T

AFTER THE GUESTS LEFT, Maggie and I wandered to the couch in the living room in a tired daze. She curled up on my lap and snuggled close to me with her eyes closed and a slight smile on her lips. I rested my hand on the curve of her slender waist. There was something calming about holding her here next to me, feeling her warmth after such an exhausting day.

Married to Irene, I would've been alone while she insisted on cleaning the kitchen above everything else. She could never let the mess sit, even when I requested she take a break. It was nice to have this quiet moment with Maggie. I liked the fact she would take the time for us. This was where the richness in life was. Being together, connecting, touching.

"When I saw how hard you were trying, I felt like you were really on my side," I said.

She frowned. "And failing. The crab was... pretty awful."

I shook my head. "Not pretty, awful."

She brightened, catching my joke. "It was truly awful."

She patted my arm and we laughed. I settled deeper into the couch, bringing Maggie's body closer to me. "I have to be honest."

Her closed eyes popped open. "Uh, oh. This can't be good."

"I... I overheard you and Rebecca talking."

She straightened on my lap. "You did?" she narrowed her eyes. "What did you hear us talking about?"

"Me. And Babbin."

"That probably wasn't good. Maybe I was a little...direct."

"You were. And he liked it. To be honest...you're the reason he decided to go with us."

She stared. Her jaw dropped. "Me? How could that be? I was such a mess."

"You worked your magic on Rebecca. Now she appreciates Babbin, and that was what he needed. There you have it."

She smiled, but it was tentative. Her gaze was steady on mine. "There we have... what? I'm good for business?"

I snuggled her back against my chest, moving her steady gaze off mine. "No, silly. You're good for me."

* * *

Maggie

Last night it took me a long time to fall asleep. The adrenaline of JT committing to an actual date had me flying high, despite the Antarctic chill I received from the women attendees. JT was able to see us as partners because I helped him score a deal. That was why he committed. That fact made me a bit nervous, though, as I wasn't sure if I could stay in the partner lane.

The sun peeked hello into my room far too early. I ignored it for as long as I could, allowing myself the luxury of lingering in my bed, but soon I couldn't do it anymore. My eyes popped opened to the bright sunlight. It was okay to get married because he saw us as partners. Right? I mean, he said "partners." Because of a business deal.

He was a businessman. He worked deals in his sleep. But that's not what really mattered here... right? He didn't see us, our relationship in terms of a deal... did he?

I pushed the worry aside. "Partners" was the word that mattered here, and the date. Celebrating *that* mattered.

I returned a congrats text to my son. Right after, my phone buzzed. Still half asleep, I pushed a button and Face-Time popped up. I found myself staring at a very large face. Dee.

"What are you doing, still waking up?" Her voice came out loud and penetrating.

I closed my eyes then opened them, and guarded myself. "Recovering."

Dee's glare seemed to penetrate the screen. "You don't have time for that. We have a wedding to plan. If we are going to rock it in August, we can't waste any time."

"How did you know about that?"

She faked gasped. "You'd think I'd be out of the know."

That had been my hope. "It happened less than ten hours ago."

"I'm good at my job."

I sat up straighter in my bed. "Apparently, or you are a creeper and secretively tapping me. There's no way—"

"I talked to JT this morning."

"Why?"

"I knew you guys were having a party last night—"

"What?"

"And he mentioned you guys had set a date."

I struggled up out of the pillows and blankets and sat up. I wasn't sure how to feel about this. Was it good that JT was already spreading the word that he was all-in on our wedding? Or was Dee honing in on things—again?

"Oka-ay," I said slowly. "Well, yes, we set a date."

"Congratulations."

"Thank you."

"I'm already scheduling the film crew for the wedding in Sedona."

"Great. Well, thanks for the update—"

"But I had an idea."

Uh oh. "An idea?"

"Yes. It'll be great."

I highly doubted Dee and I had the same definition of "great."

"What is it?" I pushed the covers back and slipped out of bed. Sunlight poured through the windows—it was going to be another scorcher. I moved out the stream of sunlight and wandered to the mini kitchen to search for a teapot.

"I thought it would be fun to shoot you and JT doing all the wedding planning—you know, shopping for dresses, picking out flowers, all the fun stuff—and we could film live responses. See you guys in action as a couple."

"That sounds… not good." I picked up my comb. My hair was almost as messy as Dee's very bad idea.

"Trust me, it'll be great."

"So, first thing to do is to figure out the next week you and JT can go up to Sedona. We need to do it soon."

I tugged on my hair. Guess I must have slept wild last night. "Dee, we'll have to get back to you on that."

It was like she didn't hear me. More likely, she didn't want to.

"What I need immediately is for you to pick your colors, let me know the kind of wedding dress you want, and the type of wedding you want to have. What do you want the mood and the experience to be?"

I thought about me and JT, all the things we were still learning about each other. Like how to move armoires. I didn't think I wanted everyone in the world to see us nego-tiating how to be together. JT would never stand for it.

"I want the mood to be romantic," I said. "And I want the experience to be private. In other words, no cameras."

"What?" Dee's shriek pierced through the phone at high speed.

"No way will JT be in favor of such a thing," I told her.

"Oh, I think I could convince him—"

"Look, Dee, we've agreed to film the actual wedding ceremony, and that's going to have to be enough."

She was silent a moment, no doubt scheming. But I wasn't even worried. There was no way JT would ever

125

agree to such a thing, and there was no way in hell Dee would be able to convince him. Win-win.

She sighed. "I'll email you guys the contract for the filming as soon as it makes it through the legal team."

"No filming the planning," I said firmly. "Hear me?"

She sighed again. "I hear you."

I squinted my eyes into the phone screen as even brighter morning light spilled into the room.

"I just sent you an email with all the information."

"Do you ever sleep?"

She laughed.

My stomach clenched.

* * *

JT

My coffee maker was chugging along slowly again this morning. I found the wait meditative. Not to Mags. She liked high speed. High drama. Noise and excitement. High heels and sparkle. We were so different. It was part of what drew me to her. I saw in her something I didn't have in me. I might need a little sparkle. A little drama. I glanced out the window at the scrub brush lining the back pasture. I sure hoped she needed a little scrub brush.

Last night everything had eventually fallen into place, despite the food debacle. Had to hand it to Maggie, she had recovered nicely, and now I had set a date to be married and was ready to charge forward on that plan.

Maggie poked her head through the sliding door. "Baby," she called out.

The warmth in her voice was endearing. "Good morning." I strolled to her and wrapped her in my arms. "I didn't expect you up at this hour."

"It's after eight," she said, confused.

"You can sleep in, you know." I ran my hand along her shoulder, liking the feel of her small body under my hand. Liking the knowledge that I could take care of her now. "You can take it easy, chill out."

Her blue eyes didn't look confused anymore. They looked... distant? "Oh, well... sure, I guess that's true." Her jaw tensed.

I cupped her chin and tipped her face up to look at mine. All I wanted was for her to feel at home here and to see the beauty of this place.

"Listen, dear," I said in a low voice, looking into her eyes. "I want you to hear me on this."

Her body swayed closer. "I'm listening." Her voice came out soft. Low. Our gazes held.

"There's nothing you need to do," I told her firmly. "Nowhere you need to be. No one needs you to do *anything* you don't want to do. I want you to relax."

Her body stiffened ever so slightly. But she smiled, which was confusing.

I walked over to the coffee maker to pour another cup into my mug. "Want one?"

She wrinkled her nose. "There's one thing I need to do for sure... get some tea in the house!"

A tea person. Right. I snatched the kettle.

"I have an idea I wanted to run by you."

I started filling up the kettle with water. "What's that?"

"I thought I could plan the whole wedding. We don't need the show to do it."

I set the kettle on the stovetop to give this thought. "But isn't planning weddings stressful?"

She puffed out her chest. "I can handle it. I want to. I want to make up for the mistakes I made last night."

I slid her tea over to her. "You landed a client last night. I say that was successful."

"Me doing the wedding could be a lot of fun."

If she wanted to do this, then I really didn't have a problem with it. Her being happy was what mattered. "If you want to."

Her head came up. "Really? I can do it my way?"

"Sure," I said.

"You would wear a white tux?"

I laughed. "I'll wear a bathing suit if you want, but not spandex. I draw my line there."

She appeared horrified, then her brow smoothed. "But you would look so good. For me, please?" She gave me a very flirty wink with a bashful smile.

"Fine. Spandex it is." I shook my head at the idea, really hoping she was teasing. I was sure she was. Well, almost positive.

"You're a very easygoing CEO."

"In the business we have here..." I moved my hand between us, "I am."

Her face poised between joyous and suspicious. "So, I can plan everything?"

Having her do it, or if the show did it, it didn't matter. As long as I didn't have to mess with it. "It's completely in your hands."

"You may live to regret that, sir," she whispered in a husky voice.

I pulled her close and kissed her, then murmured back, "Plan it right, and everything will be fine."

She stiffened in my arms as the tea kettle squealed with steam.

* * *

JT

After tea with Maggie, I met with Mr. Babbin. The meeting went quickly but well. After dropping him and his girlfriend off at the airport, my phone buzzed. Dee, again. My phone was stacking up with calls from her. Before Dee had a chance to say anything, I said, "I already told you I set a date."

"We want to shoot you preparing for the wedding."

"That's ridiculous." Dee was always trying to stir up something. It would be nice when we were no longer the flavor of the month.

"The public loves it. They'll eat it up."

I pressed harder on the gas pedal. "Nope. We'll pass. Now isn't the right time for something like that."

She cleared her throat. "I absolutely understand. You're in a tough spot, way out there with a woman like Maggie."

I lessened my foot from the gas to keep from running into the Tucson-slow car in front of me. First Babbin, now Dee. Did they know something about Maggie I wasn't seeing? "What do you mean, 'a woman like Maggie?'"

"Come on, JT, she's high-class. She used to travel the world with her last boyfriend. Parties and name brand purses and crystal. She likes glitz and glam. Got any of that out in Tucson on your pseudo-ranch? No? I bet she's already worn high heels to a barbeque, hasn't she? And fancy clothes?"

I swallowed a lump. Did Maggie travel the world with her last man? She never talked about it. But she had been complaining about Tucson. I thought she needed to get used to the change, but what if I was wrong? What if she did need more?

"JT, if Maggie is struggling at all, one of the best things you could do for her would be to bring her up to Sedona. Lots of filming and activity, cameras—heck, she can even go shopping every day. We both know she loves clothes—it would totally be her thing. She'll love it and be much more settled in the Southwest."

I stopped at a light. A biker next to me put his foot down on the pavement waiting. Bikers in Tucson always risked getting hit, riding so close to traffic. Was I risking it with Maggie trying to make her be a country person?

I had to make myself clear to Dee. "The last thing she needs is the media going after her again. I can't subject her to that."

"They won't this time. She'll be the star. America loves weddings so much, they'll completely forget anything negative in the past. Promise. That has always happened in previous shows. This is a way for her to redeem herself in the public eye."

I drummed my fingers on the steering wheel. I couldn't care less what the public thought, but it had hurt Maggie. I could see her liking a place like Sedona. "Fine, if Maggie is up for it, then I'll do it."

* * *

THE THICK, heavy, oak door snapped shut behind me, leaving me alone in my office at last. I glanced around my sanctuary at my oak bookshelves, my big screen computer flickering its screen saver, and the few papers dotting my desk with urgent issues. I would go after those once I drew up and sent the contract to Mr. Babbin. Our morning meeting had gone extremely well. Maggie had done magic with his girlfriend because I have never seen him in such a good mood. I needed to keep Maggie happy.

I closed my eyes, allowing the spinning events of last night and this morning to slip from me. I breathed in the silence, letting it fill my soul. As long as I found my quiet moments, I could do this relationship quite happily. A knock bounced against the door.

Dimitri strolled in, his expression questioning. "Well?"

"We closed the deal. The pressure is off for now."

His face relaxed and he fist-bumped me. "Good job. I had no doubt that you would do it."

Of course, he doubted. That was why he was in here within seconds of me arriving. He probably had his secretary on full lookout. "It was Maggie who convinced him."

Surprised filled Dimitri's face. "Good for her. She might be a keeper if she can close deals like that."

"I don't—"

He waved his hand to stop my protest. "I know. I know. Forget I said that. We have a lot of time-sensitive details to go over." He fingered the wood on the arm of the chair. A loud bang sounded in the hallway, diverting our attention. My office door creaked open. Two young adult boys wearing jeans and worn, black tee-shirts stumbled in loaded with heavy cameras and lights.

"Hey, Mr. JT?" one of the guys said. "Dee sent us over. We're the film crew."

My jaw dropped.

Dimitri sprung to his feet.

The guys started hauling their stuff into the office.

I stepped from behind the desk. "Hang on, who gave you permission to be here?"

"Dee."

"She doesn't own this place. She can't give permission."

The young man looked confused and a bit frightened. "But... didn't she tell you we'd be here? We're the film crew."

"I heard that part," I said grimly and turned to Dimitri. "I'm really sorry, I never gave permission..."

They bustled around us with lights and other instruments of their trade, while I tried to explain to Dimitri how our workplace was not going to be a film studio, while the young camera people were turning it into a film studio.

Dimitri stared at them as I tried to explain. I had no idea how Dee had gotten a film crew here so fast. They must have been secret agents, lodged in a Tucson Holiday Inn, waiting for their cue.

Dee was very, very good.

Dimitri didn't seem to hear much of what I was saying as they set up a reflective gadget behind my desk, but I did my best to explain anyways.

"And I agreed because I think Maggie might need more excitement than what Tucson has to offer."

Dimitri's gaze snapped to me. "Excitement? Excitement? Is that what we're aiming for now?"

"Well, not 'aiming,' but—"

"When have you ever wanted excitement, JT?"

"I—"

His face burned red. The film guys scrambled to get us on camera. I tried to guide Dimitri out of the room, but he was an immovable angry object.

"You know, JT, that show changed you. When you first went on, I thought, "Give the guy a break. He lost Irene. She was the ideal wife, quiet and supportive, perfect for him, and now she's gone." I told myself, "He needs to mix things up. That is what I told people."

"Told people? What people?"

But he was on a roll.

"But now… now this? Getting married? To someone as different from Irene as I can imagine? And a film crew?" He said the word like a curse, then stopped short. He seemed to have run out of breath. At least, he stopped. The camera was ready to record if not was already recording.

"You have every right to be upset about this. I don't blame you."

"You don't?"

"No. You did a lot to cover for me last time. You're the one who picked up the pieces. This will mean more work for you when I should be the one at least pulling my weight."

He sniffed.

I turned to the crew. "We're all done," I said stiffly to them, but Dimitri waved his hand.

We glanced at each other, hesitant.

Dimitri quickly took in the scene. "Let them shoot. You want airtime and more fame; I'm not going to stop you."

"That's not—"

He waved me off. "I know you want to get married in front of all America. Make it a spectacle."

"I actually don't want that, but it is in the contract and would cost a lot to get out of it."

Dimitri's eyes widened. "Contract?"

The loud thud of metal hitting wood sounded to my right. I looked over to the camera guy. He fumbled the boom as he picked it up.

Dimitri continued, "We made a profit last time, and I can leverage it to do the same thing this time, too. I'm never one to say no to money, even if it is for your selfish reasons."

I had no pressing need to be on TV except Dee said this was the way to keep Maggie happy.

The camera boys had established themselves in the center of my office with camera and light equipment scattered in an erratic array, reminding me of Maggie and her shoes. My eyes flicked back to Dimitri in time to catch a flash of amusement radiate across his flushed face.

The camera boys may be sloppy, but they had been lightning fast in getting the camera pointed on us.

"They're shooting. Everything you say can go on national TV."

Dimitri's chin tipped up defiantly. "Have nothing to hide."

We all have something to hide. Even my brother-in-law. I wasn't sure what he was up to, but something was off, but now wasn't the time to ask.

I strolled over to the camera guy and hovered over him to make my point. "This is the last of the filming you'll be doing here in Tucson. The rest will have to wait until Sedona. We prep the wedding there. You film us there." The camera boy gulped before nodding in compliance.

That done, I went back to Dimitri. "Okay," I ventured, "how do you want to handle this?"

He edged closer to me and said, "Best man."

"What?"

"You make me your 'best man.'"

The camera boys shuffled in the room, probably for a close-up. Of course, he would be the best man. Who else would I ask? I threw up my hands. "Okay. If that's what you want... That was the plan all along anyway."

He slapped me on my back.

Only then did I notice the gel in his hair and his well-pressed, pale-blue dress shirt.

"Dimitri, are your trying to get a woman?"

Looking straight at the camera with large puppy dog eyes, he said, "If the right one came along, I wouldn't complain."

* * *

BY LUNCH TIME, I hurried home to tell Maggie the "good" news about the show we were going to star in. After the garage door closed, I climbed out of my car to see Maggie standing in the garage shaking like a delicate leaf.

"The neighborhood cat has a squirrel in his mouth," she said, running out of breath. "He's right outside the glass door. He won't stop going from one sliding door to the other with it."

"Ahh, it brought you a present."

Her eyes widened. "Well, I could do without them." She jumped into my arms.

Her whole form trembled and I kissed her forehead to try to calm her. "It's okay, sweetheart. The cat loves you."

"I don't want to be loved that much." She wiped at her eyes and gave me a funny look. "What are you doing home?"

"I came for lunch."

Her brows furrowed. "Canned soup?"

I smiled at the great idea. "Sure."

I followed her into the kitchen, and we quickly threw together a lunch with crackers and soup. Once we sat at the dining room table, I rested the spoon on the edge of the bowl. "I have good news."

Her eyes flickered. "What?"

"Dee called me and asked me if we would be willing to have a show shoot of us prepping our wedding in Sedona."

"She called you, too?" Maggie broke tiny cracker crumbs into her soup.

"I've arranged it so that we'll be going up there in week to get our wedding rocking."

Maggie set down her cracker on the dinner plate. "I thought we agreed that I would plan our wedding."

I smiled. "I know. But this way, you won't have to worry about anything, and you'll get to go shopping without the limitation of what's available in Tucson."

Maggie didn't meet my eye. "True."

CHAPTER 9

Maggie

A WEEK after Dee called JT, we hopped in the car and headed to Sedona to shoot the marriage prep and then the actual wedding. I should have been clicking my high heels together in excitement over it, but instead, it didn't sit well with me. JT had charged ahead and made agreements with Dee without discussing it with me. He was so used to being in charge, that was his way. I didn't say anything. But still…

I shrugged off the thought and glanced at the speedometer. Maybe my unease wasn't about keeping quiet, maybe it was JT's driving speed. The needle hovered at about five miles an hour. I walked in heels faster than this.

It was going to take forever to reach Sedona. "What are you doing?"

"Watching out for the critters." His eyes focused on the

road. He stepped on the brakes hard, which propelled me forward the seatbelt snapping down hard on me.

"What was that?"

"A lizard."

He had to be kidding. "Am I marrying a modern-day male Snow White?"

The muscles around his eyes twitched, but he said nothing. I rubbed at my neck. "My neck hurts."

He reached over and squeezed my hand. "Sorry about that. Are you okay?"

I nodded.

"I'm going slow because if I go faster, I'll have to hit the brakes harder, and that's how I broke your table on the trip in. You choose."

Breathe, I told myself but, instead of breathing, I blurted out, "JT, I know you like to be in control, but I think it's a better idea if I drive, and you relax in the passenger side from all your hard work."

"Nope."

I sighed. "Could you at least put people before animals?"

"Yes, sweetheart. You'll always come first. I'll try to be more gentle on the brakes."

An edge of a smile danced on his lips. He stopped for a light as bikers dressed in matching red racing outfits gathered near my window, ready to race us to the next light. As if we were racing them toward our wedding.

I watched the road, letting the hypnotic quality of riding in a car do its work. The days had been exhausting since I arrived in Tucson, with me unpacking, then launching into a major project of redecorating the guesthouse, and trying to make friends with the neighbors by going to lunches and joining book clubs.

I thought of everything that had been happening as the road spread out before me in a hypnotic way. I must have fallen asleep because the ringing of a phone jolted me awake. I rubbed my eyes, noting that the landscape had completely transformed into long stretches of open land.

My phone rang again. I hunted for it and finally saw it on the floor by my feet. "Hello." I answered, sitting up straighter in the car seat.

"Where are you?" came Dee's insistent voice. "The camera crew's not answering. I don't think they have cell reception."

I blinked at the glaring sunlight. "In the middle of nowhere."

"Were setting up everything for you to choose the cake, and we'll have somebody shooting you two driving into town."

I sat upright in my chair. They were going to start shooting in an hour. I flipped down the sun visor mirror and a nervous tingle shot through my stomach. Dee continued rattling off the packed schedule as I fluffed my hair, and touched up my makeup. There wasn't going to be much downtime. My mouth had gone dry. I took a drink from the water bottle.

The moment I ended the call, JT asked, "What was that about?" He used almost the same tone as Dee had. It must be one of those business things.

"Cake choosing, and shooting the car driving into town."

"You… have got… to be… kidding me. We don't even have time to settle in?"

"No, we're going to get the show started."

JT stared straight at the road, the muscles in his face flinching.

I bit my lip. "I think you were right about agreeing to do the show even though I wasn't happy about it at first. It's going to be fun to plan the wedding, and why not share it with our fans?"

We passed several mileage markers without a word as the tires hummed against the road. He drummed his finger on the steering wheel. "Good point. I just really wanted a nap after this driving."

I stared out at the road winding through the mountain pass. "Are we okay?"

He took a quick glance from looking at the road across to me. "Why wouldn't we be?"

I shrugged.

"Something must be getting at *you*. You're snappy and not talking much." I stared at the desert bushes as we drove by. After a drawn-out silence, I said, "It seems like you are mad at me."

"Not mad. I'm driving."

I swallowed and glanced away. "You can't drive and talk?"

"Hey, come on." He reached out and touched my arm. "What gives?"

I shifted in the seat to face him. "You have been really quiet, so you must be mad."

He drummed his fingers on the steering wheel. "How do you get that I'm mad when I'm only just driving?"

"Growing up, quiet meant I did something wrong."

"That's messed up."

It was messed up. My mom like to take off a lot, but I wasn't going to talk about it, and JT wasn't going to leave me.

He took my hand in his. His touch was warm, comforting. He was still here. He hadn't kicked me to the curb, or yelled, or turned around to drop me off.

He gave my hand a squeeze. "Maggie, I'm not going to leave you because you don't 'perform' for me."

That might not be completely true. Maybe he believed that was how he was, but he'd said very clearly the reason we picked a wedding date was because I'd performed *very* well. And if a good performance could win me a wedding, what could a bad one lose me?

He squeezed my hand again. "I'm still here."

"Why were *you* so upset?"

"Dee is always so intrusive. Would it really hurt her to give us a few hours to at least arrive at the destination before shooting? She arrived a day or two early so she could rest. She should give us the same courtesy. I was hoping to get away from everything to spend at least a day in the mountains together. It would appear Dee is determined to not allow that to happen."

"Maybe we still can get away," I offered, hoping that idea didn't include camping.

* * *

JT

My shoulders relaxed the farther away we were from

Tucson. Dimitri had been extra unrelenting in work-machine mode. I pulled the car onto the freeway heading north with Maggie at my side. The quietness of the car wrapped around me like an unfamiliar blanket. The sky was a deep blue with the only clouds being small white puffs surfacing above the distant mountain range. Scrappy-looking trees and bushes dotted the desert landscape. I leaned back in the car seat with the air conditioner fan on high as the hours passed, focusing on nothing but the road ahead. My peace was only slightly disturbed by Dee's meddling. This wedding show was beginning to appeal more to me.

America would now see me driving on these almost deserted roads as the camera crew followed us and sometimes raced ahead to capture B-roll. It would be nice when I was not followed around with a camera, but for now, it was okay because it would make Maggie happy... right? We were certainly different, but I loved having her by my side.

I rolled down my window to let the desert smells in. The road had become curvy and took more focus.

In two dozen years of working with some of the highest-level management corporate clients and partners, I'd learned that people were a lot more willing to work with you if they were well fed and well rested. Oh, with Maggie, it might also include shopping.

I smiled at the long highway winding away before us. Maybe I did know what to do in this relationship, after all. I reached for Maggie's hand on the seat beside me. "I was thinking..."

"Uh oh," she said. I took her hand and covered it with mine on my thigh.

"I thought maybe you'd like a spa day when we get there." I turned a beaming smile her way.

"What? A spa day?"

My beaming smile faltered. "Um, yes?"

"A whole day?"

"Well, I thought—"

She turned in her seat and faced me full on, her eyes bright and intent. "Do you know what we have to do when we get there? We have a *wedding* to plan. We need flowers, and a dress, tux, and oh man, the venue! And we'll need…"

I glanced at the highway then back at her. She listed off a whole lot of to do's. We would be way too busy but, for some reason, Maggie didn't sound stressed. She sounded… like she was looking forward to all this planning and shopping.

Soon, the landscape changed from cactus, hills, and brown dirt to stunning red soil. The red started out as a subtle hint with a light dusting on the ground in-between more greenery. When I rounded the corner, large jagged red buffs filled up the real estate. The street signs changed to names like Horse Thief Basin, Bloody Basin Road, Coffee Pot Drive, and Chimney Rock. This was my kind of country.

Maggie wasn't even looking at the beauty before her. Instead, she was fixing her makeup, letting all the beauty pass her by. A sadness weighed me down when I reflected about her childhood. It must have been hard.

"Pit stop in two minutes," I said.

"Oh, good. Where're my shoes?" She looked around the seat.

"Are you going to want anything in the convenience store?"

"A hug."

She needed a lot more reassurance than Irene ever did. But then, Irene came from a quiet, privileged background, and moved into one with our marriage. Maggie was different, but that was exactly what I wanted. I wanted to take all the burdens off her. Let her know she was fine as she was, and didn't need to do anything. I'd have to remind her she didn't need to work now.

"I can do that." I glanced at the clock. We were making good time. "By the way, did your childhood have something to do with you running away on the show?"

Her hand, holding a makeup brush, froze halfway to her face, then sank to her lap. Her head lowered. "Where did that come from?"

"I've just been thinking about it, and what it must have been like to have a mom like yours. I'm wondering if it makes it harder to trust people, and if that was why things happened the way they did on the show."

Her face had tightened, her forehead a tapestry of furrows. Her hand clenched around her hairbrush. I felt a spark of anger emanating from her, too.

"Hey, Maggie? I want to understand you better. Me not talking doesn't mean anything other than I'm not talking, and I'm not as verbal as you."

"Or you are disconnecting and not telling anyone about it," she shot out.

I sighed. She wasn't going to let me solve this problem and move on. I pulled the car up to the gas station.

Maggie scrambled for her shoes. I hopped out and hurried around the car to open the door for her and give her a hug. She took a few more moments gathering her purse before climbing into my arms.

"Baby, I love you." She wrapped her arms tightly around me.

"I love you too—"

Before I could say any more to patch up the uncomfortable hiccup, someone called, "There's Maggie Chambers and JT Devonshire!"

A group of middle-aged women dressed in swooping long tops with wild cotton prints buzzed with each other and pointed in our direction from a car in the next lane. I closed my eyes to find strength for crazy fans.

The tallest lady, towering over the others by at least a foot, headed straight in our direction. "I can't believe it's you guys. You two make the cutest couple!"

I stepped back from her toward the gas pump.

Maggie grabbed me, stood on her tippy toes, and kissed me on my scruffy cheek.

The ladies squealed. The tallest took the lead and stepped up to Maggie. "I was always rooting for you, Maggie. I just knew that you were perfect for JT, unlike my friends back there."

She thumbed toward the group of women who had huddled in tighter to each other. "I told them that you had *life*. Passion. Spunk." The woman glanced up at me, then back to Maggie. "JT needs spunk. Oh, what's her name was sweet and kind and very beautiful, but she couldn't make a man feel alive."

She even had the nerve to wink at me. "Aren't I right?"

I put the gas pump into the car. Passion. Spunk. Maggie certainly had that.

Maggie tugged on my arm. "You like my spunk?" She batted her eyes repetitively at me until I burst into laughter.

"Most of the time."

"Seriously!" Maggie rolled her eyes.

The fan laughed as the other ladies came up, muttering "hi's" and "nice to meet you's."

"So," a bright-red haired short lady spoke up, "when is the big day?"

Maggie flipped her gaze back up me with more than a playful expression. She was asking if I was still in.

"Ladies," I said with my hand extended like I was trying to heal the crowd, "you'll have to see."

Maggie slapped me on the chest with the back of her hand. "Baby, stop all your teasing. These ladies are going to get the wrong impression." She smiled, and addressed the group again, "If I were you, just between us, I'd keep your eyes on the news for an announcement."

The ladies squealed, gasped, and brought their hands to their lips. "That's so exciting. We sure will."

She leaned into the circle before I could think how to respond. "Shh, remember it's a secret between us, okay?"

I stared back at the pump. Maggie did like all this attention. She seemed to come alive with those fans. Maybe Dee had been right, and Tucson wasn't going to be enough to keep her happy.

CHAPTER 10

 T

ONCE WE ARRIVED in Sedona and settled into the meeting with Dee, I couldn't help but think that lady was destined for a cardiac arrest. I didn't know a person who was more wigged out than her. Even though she dressed up and wore makeup, she couldn't hide the black shadows or the puffiness under her eyes. Even though she was in her late twenties, early thirties, her neck jetted forward, her shoulders slumped, and her back bent over in all the wrong places. The weight of TV production had pounded her into the ground.

This was exactly what I *didn't* want for Maggie. I wanted to relieve all the stress and tension she'd had in her life, but instead of relieving the tension, we had to have our first meeting with Dee and the production crew. It took place in Maggie's hotel room. Dee had left and returned with an armful of magazines, books, and papers, and a fake smile over gritted teeth. I had rarely, if ever, seen her smile naturally.

"Wedding planning time," she sang out.

"Dee, what are you doing?" I asked.

She nodded to the camera and said pleasantly, "Let's choose wedding colors."

Her armful of books tumbled into a sofa and she pulled out what looked like a painter's paint samples. "You can have any color you want. What will it be?" She handed me one wheel, and Maggie another. She whispered "work with me here," through her teeth as though it wouldn't be picked up by the cameras.

I spread open the color fan and sighed. "I am no good at this stuff." I tossed the wheel on the table. "Dear," I looked at Maggie who had already dived into the samples. "Why don't you pick? You did a great job with redecorating the guesthouse." I went to stand up, and Dee suddenly appeared behind me, forcing me to sit back down.

"Maggie needs you by her side," she whispered at me.

I slumped back in my seat. Guess I wasn't going anywhere. I looked miserably over at Maggie, who flipped through the colors, brow knitted, lips pursed.

"This is so hard." Maggie ran her fingers over the colors. "There are endless possibilities. So many choices that could create so many moods and send very different messages to the world. JT, what mood do you want?"

Boom. The cameras flipped over to focus on me with prying, intrusive eyes. I shrugged. "Whatever you want."

Her nose wrinkled. "This is so much fun. Don't you love we can create whatever we want?"

I'd never thought about it that way before. To me, it was all stress and hassle, something to be managed. But Maggie was happy, so I guess I'd done my job. "I want what will make you happy."

She swished her lips back and forth. "It'll depend on where we have the wedding. We want the colors to compliment the ambiance."

I slumped. Ambiance? Ambiance was going to take forever.

"She's right." Dee piped in for no apparent reason other than to say something.

Maggie continued to flip through the color fan. "No grays. That color is dreadfully depressing."

Gray's depressing? It was one of my favorites. "Whatever you think, will be fine."

"Fine? Fine?" Her voice rose an octave as she spoke.

I looked over to Dee for help, but that was a mistake. She was nodding in agreement in support of Maggie.

"Ladies, I've gotta be honest, colors aren't in my wheelhouse. The two colors we choose with cell towers are brown or green. Unless you want one of those—"

"No," Maggie said with a short quick bite.

"Then you pick the color."

Dee stormed into the scene. "JT," she said with her hands on her hips in a disapproving matter like I had been a bad boy. "We need you more involved in *your* wedding."

She was trying to shame me on national television. She was angling this like I didn't care about my wedding. She was trying to plant ideas into Maggie's head, and I wasn't going to put up with that.

"Dee, stop spinning this. Of course, I care about my wedding. Maggie is just great with it. She just redecorated my entire guesthouse and did a stunning job. I trust her choices." I pointed my finger at Dee. "Don't make this more than it is."

* * *

Maggie

Dee proceeded to drill us with so many wedding questions, it made my head whirl. "Do you want a lot of guests or a few? What kind of ceremony do you want? Want a priest or a justice of the peace? Flower girls or keep it simple?"

My throat constricted. This was becoming real. Marriage was such a huge commitment. JT didn't seem so happy. I turned to him and said, "You seem grouchy."

He hesitated, then waved his hand at the film crew arrayed around us and the color wheel on the table. "I don't like all this show stuff. People make such a big deal about the wedding. The focus should be on the marriage. I prefer real joy and connection."

I wiped the sweat on the palms of my hands onto my pant leg. "This is part of real connection." My voice came out constrained and tight. "Are you against this?"

"I am here, aren't I?"

I flipped my hair onto my back. I needed to get things back in a good spot with JT. We exchanged a pensive look.

Dee strolled over to me and whispered. "Don't burden him. You don't want him to take off."

Those words punched me in the chest. Hard. My head whirled as JT grabbed my hand, and pulled me up, heading to my hotel room.

"I want to talk without anyone recording." He scurried around the small room, scoping it out to make sure we were alone, without camera people. During his search, he spotted a camera bolted up in a high corner of the sitting room. He ripped it down and flung it outside the door.

I stared at him.

He shrugged at me. "I'll buy a new one." He stood with his feet apart like he was about to tackle someone. "This is getting out of control."

I swallowed. "What exactly? Why are you irritated?"

"Are you saying I'm not doing enough for you?" His voice rose.

"I'm not saying that. Where did that come from? I just asked why you're irritated. Coming here and doing this show was your idea. Not mine."

"But I did it for you."

I stared at him. "What?"

"Dee told me you wouldn't be happy in Tucson, and Sedona would be more what you would want."

I covered my eyes with my hands trying to take in what he was saying. "Baby, I was fine with Tucson. I care more about being with you than the town I am in. I was actually looking forward to planning it myself. I wanted to do it for you … for us…"

"Then why were you acting funny at home?"

"What?" I tried to scan my memory for what he could

possibly talking about. "Maybe it's because you have a lot of memories of your past relationships around."

"What?"

I shrugged, not wanting to go into it. "It just makes me feel like you haven't let go."

"Sorry about that. I meant to clean it up. I got distracted. I will get to it." His shoulders slumped. "I thought I was failing you. Irene was never happy with me. I could never do enough to keep her satisfied. I thought I was failing again."

I lowered my voice. "Well, you win with me."

A smile cracked on the side of his mouth. "Really?"

I smiled wide. "Really. Now, I know you've had an intense schedule lately. Let's do something fun. How about skydiving?" I dashed a glance at the clock. "We could still make it today if we rushed."

He scratched his head. "What are you talking about?" He began to pace around my hotel room like a caged dog.

I shrugged. "You seemed cooped up."

He sighed. "I do need to get outside." He paused his pacing to peer out the window.

I walked over to him. We stood together and looked out at the mountains.

He reached out to me and pulled me close. "Sweetheart, thanks, I'm fine. Really. A moment of irritation. A flash-back. I'm over it."

"Let's get you into nature as soon as we can."

Our hands entwined, and we stood quietly for a while. We both jumped when the crew burst into the room and flocked around us.

"We picked sage green with a light rose as an accent," I said.

Dee nodded. "That will work. Glad, we got that done. Now we need to get to cake picking."

Seven minutes later, we found ourselves in a hotel meeting room with samples of cake spread out before us. Cameras pointed at us with their green lights on.

"Cake. Let's talk cake." Dee slapped her hand on the flipping table making it wobble between us. "What flavor?"

I closed my eyes for a moment to put on "show Maggie." After taking a few deep breaths, I opened my eyes, smiled, and said, "Chocolate. The darker, the richer, the better. Hmm." I smacked my lips together. "JT want to have your favorite flavor to go in-between?" Before I said more, I realized I had just made an assumption. "That is if you like chocolate."

JT looked around the room, dazed. Probably wishing he was in the mountains, not this room with velvet-lined wallpaper and silver and gold accents. I knew what it felt like to be somewhere you didn't fit—Tucson—so I sympathized. Better give him a moment.

I stepped forward and said brightly. "Okay, how about... a chocolate fountain on a table in the middle of the room in addition to the chocolate cake."

Dee gave a fake yawn. "Bor-r-ring."

JT's face held its normal stoicism, but I suspected, underneath, anger brewed. He didn't flinch, just let Dee and me bounce ideas back and forth like we were champion tennis players. I wished JT and I could really talk without the cameras and work out our disagreement, which at this point

I wasn't even sure *I* understood. If we couldn't talk about it, he could at least add something to the conversation so I could have a good idea if we were headed in the right direction.

I swished my lips back and forth. JT needed my prompting, whether he'd ever say so or not. "Your grandchildren would love the chocolate. They sure went after it at the family reunion last year."

That caught his attention. I couldn't exactly read what he thought, but I saw a twitch around his eyes and sensed an increased tenderness toward me. If I wasn't mistaken, the hard anger that had drawn his jaw tight, also slackened.

Dee flipped through her folders until she found the piece of paper she wanted. "Here's the picture of the cake they'll do for you. They'll allow slight variations, but this is what it'll be." She slid over a picture. "It's a little over four feet tall. They'll put silk pearls on the cake for decoration."

The column of cake was tiered. The icing was an off-white with small petals on top of each tier. Each one of the petals came from the type of flowers JT had handed out to other girls on the show. Red frosting circled around the entire bottom layer of the cake with the *Millionaire Engagement* heart logo featured with prominence.

I tossed the photo back at Dee. "That is not happening."

"But—" Dee started to say.

I leaned into the table to make sure she heard me. "I am not going to have a cake at *my* wedding celebrating all the flowers JT gave out on the show to other women!" My heart pounded hard. I struggled to catch my breath. "Seriously, no self-respecting woman would stand for that on her day. I want my cake, *our* cake, to be about us, not all the others."

"If Maggie's upset, it doesn't happen," JT said firmly.

By this point, I had started to shake and JT's arm suddenly surrounded me, tugging me toward him.

I looked up at him. "They want symbols of your ex-girl-friends on our cake!"

"Not happening."

Thank heavens, JT was on my side. He would see to it that it wouldn't happen.

Armed with JT's support, I yanked out my phone from my pocket, pulled up Google, and began searching. I wasn't going to stop pushing this idea of chocolate. Dee wanted big. She was going to have it. A quick search told me the largest chocolate fountain wedding cake was twenty-six feet and three inches tall. It circulated two tons, or 4,409 pounds of chocolate, at the rate of 120 quarts per minute. The fountain would flow higher than some office buildings with dark melted chocolate falling with a roar louder than a waterfall.

When I told all this to Dee, she frowned. "Twenty-six feet... with children. That's a huge liability risk."

JT's hand remained on my back. He still said nothing, but caressed me in soothing strokes.

I really wasn't sure what JT wanted. I did know I'd never go for the propaganda cake for my wedding, especially hinting at other women. Not happening. "Four feet high then."

Dee smacked her lips together. "Done." She pointed her finger at me. "Don't you go and Google the most expensive cake now, too."

I laughed at her and did exactly that, likely following her intended ploy. She was milking a good scene out of us for the cameras without even trying, but I didn't care. I was going to have the wedding the way JT and I wanted it. Big. Memorable. That would make him happy, right? I would give his clients and employees something to talk about. This wedding would be such an amazing experience no one would remember the food I cooked at JT's barbecue.

"Here it is!" I showed her the screen on my phone and shared it with JT. "It's only $20 million and has eight tiers with more than 4,000 diamonds on it. The wedding party plans to eat it!"

I looked at Dee with my eyebrows raised. This was her department since the show footed the bill.

JT's eye caught mine. They held a mischievous glint. "I love it," he said. He knew I was poking at Dee.

Dee paled. "I'm not pitching a diamond wedding cake to my producers."

I sighed in mock drama. "Fine. I'll have to get by without eating diamonds."

JT laughed. "But that would've been a spectacular experience, eating diamonds. Though the digestion would be rough." He patted his stomach.

Thank heavens for JT. He got it. That meant no matter what the nasty viewers said, he understood me. I wanted that. I needed that. To poke back at Dee for that horrible cake idea, I said, "I guess you're going to say no to having diamonds on my dress, too."

"That reminds me, I have exciting news. You're going to love it."

She pulled out a business card and waved it like the flag lady at a racetrack. "Brian Caledre, the all-star of all-star designers, has agreed to allow you to select your wedding dress from his collection."

She waited for my response.

I had none.

"Ooh! Isn't that the coolest? Brian. Seriously, you can't get cooler than him."

Did Dee, who wore holey jeans and three-day-old clothes, care about fashion?

"Are you getting a kickback for marketing his brand?"

She flinched at my comment. "No. He's a friend."

"How good of a friend?"

Dee flushed. "He's offered his team's services, and the studio has taken him up on it."

I eyed Dee, suspecting she might have a crush on this designer. Dee had never once shown even the slightest interest in fashion, and now she was gushing. That was funny.

"We only do this if Maggie wants it," JT said.

Dee rolled her eyes.

* * *

JT

Sitting in a fabric covered chair at the small, but nicely finished, wooden desk in my hotel room, my head pounded as I stared at the wrinkled bed. Today had been rough. I wrung my hands together. Next time I came to Sedona, I'd bring my horses. I'd find a stable and go on a trail ride at dusk. Maggie might even like it. My mind pictured her on a horse. Okay, maybe not.

I took a sip from a water bottle. Today on set, I had

exploded on camera. America would see it. I had never done anything like that before. That behavior had to stop.

Ever since Maggie had moved into my house, nothing had been the same, not even the clean counters. Everything swirled around her, including my patience, and that was odd for me.

Seeing Maggie's jaw tighten was amazingly attractive. I liked that she didn't flinch. Instead, she had fired back at me that I was being unreasonable. In this case, she might have a point.

I stood and paced the room. Her eyes had become so wide and full of tears as she pointed out I was surrounding her with all the stuff from my past relationships. Besides the cookbooks, I wasn't sure what she was talking about, but she had a lot of feelings about it. That, and me not talking on our drive up. If she wanted me to talk, if she wanted my opinion, fine, she would get it.

* * *

Maggie

"How do you imagine the ceremony going?" Dee asked. "We really need a band. Something big, big, big."

I stared at her. "Oh-h, good question. I don't know." I laughed, shocked to realize I had given my dress more thought than the ceremony. "Is it bad I have no idea what JT would like?"

Dee shrugged. "You are still getting to know each other."

"But I want him to remember our wedding with good memories, not grimaces."

"Good goal." Dee tapped her finger on the table, "I don't know JT as well as you, but I do know wealthy men often care about the cool experience. The unique event that's different from everyone else's."

I didn't know if JT was like that. "JT did go on this show to find a wife," I thought out loud. "So, what makes Sedona different from everywhere else?"

Dee shot back. "Red dirt."

I thought about that. "There are other places like that in southern Utah."

Dee pointed her finger at me. "Vortexes!"

"Perfect," I clapped my hands together. "This will be so cool and different. We could get married in the middle of a vortex."

"But that's not visual," Dee pointed out. "It won't translate to TV well. He won't be able to brag as much if the viewer doesn't experience it."

I leaned back in my chair. That was true. "If going big would make JT happy, then going big would be what we'd do.

"Fine. Do it on a stunning mountain top where the vortex has a strong current. Floating on a hot air balloon."

"With violins," Dee added.

I snapped my fingers and pointed at her. "Yes, with violins. This is going to be so great. This will truly blow JT away, and that was what mattered, even if floating in a hot air balloon did sound I little nerve-wracking.

* * *

I WOKE with the soft golden rays slipping into my room in thin slivers of light teasing me awake. A half hour later, the quiet morning traveled with me into JT's room. Faint noises of the maids cleaning an upper floor sounded above us. Heat penetrated through the foam coffee cup I brought for JT, burning my fingers. I now knew life for him didn't begin without a cup, and maybe me getting him one would mend things over from my outburst last night.

I flushed, thinking about how petty I must have appeared complaining about being surrounded by other women's belongings. The entire nation was going to look at me as a jealous woman. Insensitive, too. My stomach clenched as I thought about the upcoming attacks. It was his dead wife's belongings that I raged about the most. She had died of cancer. He loved her. I needed to learn how to deal with that.

He stood from the desk to greet me with a crooked, guilty smile. His wet hair slicked back and his pale blue T-shirt made his eyes pop, which made my knees weak. The hotel room smelled like a clean man fresh from a morning shower. I inhaled. He approached me and my heartbeat picked up.

I held out the coffee to him trying to keep my hand steady. "I brought your favorite coffee, just the way you like it."

He took a sip. The jitters in my stomach increased. Did he like it? Did I make it right? What the heck… I was more nervous in the relationship with him now than when I chased him and played the "pick me" dance on the show.

JT cautiously sipped his coffee. "Thanks. I could get used to a cup like this already made every day."

I shook my head. "I could get used to you making me tea, too."

He chuckled. "We'll see." He shifted his weight. "Where to?"

Pleased he liked my coffee and seemed more relaxed, I glanced at my watch. "The schedule said picking a wedding dress, then picking rocks."

"What does 'picking rocks' mean?"

"Little rocks with energy stored in them."

He looked shocked. "What?"

"I know it's a bit weird."

"Yes, it is."

"I don't want to do it but I really don't want to go to battle with Dee about this."

"I'll do it."

I put my hand on his chest to hold him back. "Oh-h, I do find this protective side of you very attractive." I lifted my eyebrows up and down. "But, let's save our ammunition for when it matters."

He looked like he wanted to continue to fight, but clenched his jaw instead. "So, we'll let them do the energy rocks. Deal?"

I smiled back. "Deal."

"Are you okay picking out a dress with me? I know most men hate shopping, and grooms think it's bad luck to see the bride in her dress before the wedding."

"I'm not superstitious. Besides, you need someone there for you, and that's my job."

He took my hand and squeezed it. I squeezed his back. Then he tipped his head forward and kissed me gently on the mouth, making everything all better.

"Let's go do this thing." His mouth hovered an inch away from my lips.

"Right. Really, we don't need to care, do we?"

He shook his head. "This is their thing. Ours is what's to come."

Warmth poured through my chest. "Our marriage," I whispered.

He kissed me again, creating sparks through my whole body. He pulled away and held my gaze for a long moment, then we turned toward the door.

"It's all an act anyhow," I assured him. "Isn't that what you said? Weddings are just for show."

He swung the door open. "Isn't everything?" He ushered me through the door.

I stopped short and looked up at him. "But not us, right? We're not an act?"

"Not even close."

That settled the rising worry in my chest, and I smiled at him.

We kept holding hands as we hurried downstairs. Oozing with happiness, we made our way to the hotel meeting room where dresses had magically appeared.

Rows and rows of dresses hung, flowing and glittering in various artistic shapes and forms. Under dim lights, with spotlights glowing on the gowns, soft violin music soared in the background. An absolutely gorgeous woman with long hair, dark skin, and at least six-inch heels strolled over to us.

The camera zoomed in on her runway model strut with her silky duster trailing behind. The duster slipped off of one shoulder, accented by a long thick stream of pearls. A rich musky scent surrounded us as she extended her long elegant hand. I shook it, barely touching her fingertips.

"I'm Pearl, the star of *The Dress.* We're going to find you a perfect gown."

Great. Of course. Nice one, Dee. Put me next to Ms. Perfect, I-look-good-in-anything, to find my dress.

JT offered his hand too eagerly, if you ask me. "Nice to meet you."

She peeked up at him under her long, thick black eyelashes. "I loved you on the show. I watched it every Monday night."

My grip on his arm tightened. "How are we going to find this perfect dress?"

The model stepped back and clapped her hands together. "You're playing a game. You both will start at different sides of the room. You have ten minutes to select *the* dress you think is the best one for your wedding."

JT's jaw tightened. Guess he'd thought he could get away with being an observer. No luck, cowboy.

The Beauty Queen cleared her throat. "We want to see how you two imagine the big day. It's like a test to see if you two are on the same page."

JT rubbed his hands as if preparing for something. "The person in the dress is all I care about."

I gave him a stupid, silly, schoolgirl grin. Pearl smiled, too. I scowled at her as she kept giving us instructions. "You'll pick *the* one. We're working with your gut instinct. No choice will be wrong, since they are all originals."

I peered over at the gowns to see if I could get a sneak peek. "I do love the idea of being an original."

"This is a recipe for failure." JT had taken several steps

away from me, which happened to be nearer to the exit. "If I pick the wrong color or size, I'll be headed for a major chew-out, or plagued with questions of how fat do you think I am? Or, skinny. Either way, I lose."

I grabbed hold of JT's sleeve to gain his attention and reassure him. "Don't worry about size or color. I can find the right one after this, look more for the style you think would flatter me."

JT pursed his lips, then nodded. "I can do that."

"I believe in you," I teased.

We grinned at each other, and some of that earlier warmth we had between us splashed back. We could do this as a team, even if they purposely split us up.

Pearl glided to JT with her long hair flowing. "Don't worry. I'm your secret weapon. I'll help you." She winked at him.

Seriously, she winked. That woman needed to back away from my man.

JT blushed.

A horn blared, signaling a time for us to separate. I strolled down an aisle to my left as JT took off with Pearl at his side. I glanced at him, hoping to catch his gaze, but he didn't look back. Instead, he walked with his head tilted down listening to Pearl.

That was fine. His mind was on me. He wouldn't be swayed by a model. He loved me even with my puffy eyes from my earlier crying episode. I brushed my bangs behind my ear. It's nothing.

A line of gowns was displayed as individual showpieces. There were long, straight silky dresses with high cuts along the thigh, and large southern bell dresses. Others featured short trains, and others sported plunging neck lines. My head hurt as I gazed down the line at all of them. I could just imagine what it was like for JT. He had been clueless picking a hot tub, and this was shopping on a whole new level.

To JT, this was part of the act, the show, but symbols mattered, and this dress would be a statement to the world that JT and I belonged together. Which dress would be the ticket? Some dresses were sewn with a lot of handmade beads. Some had diamonds, reminding me of my very bad jokes last night about the diamond cake.

How to choose? I rounded a row then saw, in the corner, a deep red-silk gown with a sleek form-fitting hourglass shape. The sleeves were formed from a delicate lace. A red ruby belt in the shape of a triangle flattered the waist. The slender bodice rippled with romantic wrinkles down into a pile of cascading ruffles that collected and tumbled to the ground, flaring out in a large swoop, which emphasized the slender waist. A chapel train extended from the ruffles to add to the glamour.

That was my dress. I couldn't wait to try it on.

Now to reclaim my guy from Miss Beauty Queen.

* * *

JT

There are few things that men hate more than being stuck in a room full of dresses, but being forced to pick out the wedding gown for my intended with a model by my side was definitely worse.

Pearl sauntered up to me and hooked her arm into the

crease of my elbow. I straightened my arm, shook her hand off and stepped farther away from the troublemaker.

"Maggie wouldn't appreciate that, Pearl."

Her fingers returned and lingered on my forearm as I struggled to not step on any of the gowns that they'd spread out and caught me like cactus needles. A camera zoomed up tight on me. I took a few more steps, then grabbed a gown with lace and beads.

Pearl wrapped her hand over mine. "That dress is designed for someone like me, with a long waist. Maggie has a short one. She would look," Pearl wrinkled her nose, "heavier."

The final whispered word made me release my hand from the hanger. I knew full well the editors could make more of what just happened than what actually happened. I stepped back and examined the dress to consider what Pearl had said.

As the whistle blew to signal time was up, I had looked at what seemed like hundreds of dresses, and my headache had only deepened.

Pearl bellowed for us to gather at the back of the room. Each gown I had chosen was on display with mood lights cast on each to bring out their best features.

"Wow," Pearl said. "You must have picked at least twenty gowns."

I shrugged. "What can I say? Maggie would be stunning in any of them." I turned to a crew member standing next to me. "Can I get some aspirin?"

They took off running to serve me. Feeling guilty to be waited on like that, I looked up to see Maggie rounding the corner carrying a red dress.

"Red?"

"It's nontraditional. Trendy," Pearl whispered from the side of her mouth.

She turned and instructed Maggie where to stand for the next scene. Maggie hopped onto her designated spot, then looked over in my direction. When her gaze landed on me, she smiled so big it filled her whole face. She blew passionate kisses my way.

Leave it to her to find a way to be quirky and lighten the moment. I chuckled and blew one back.

"Now, for the second part of the activity." Pearl completely played to the cameras...standing just so and winking into the lens. "From the looks of things, it'll be easier for Maggie than JT."

Perfect.

Pearl drew out the tension for an unnaturally long time before telling us what this activity would be. I had long ago learned it was a trick they used for television.

"Out of your collection of dresses, I want you to pick the perfect dress. *The* dress for the wedding in which she will say, 'I do,' in front of all America."

Would this ever end?

The assistant snapped up a curtain between Maggie and me so we could surprise the other person with our gown choice.

The moment the curtain was completely up, I asked, "Where's Dee?"

The young girl looked at me with fear in her eyes. "Why?"

"Get her here now."

She jumped and left the room. Three minutes later, Dee

strolled in wearing her backwards baseball cap, shredded jeans, and a purple shirt. "You rang?"

"You pick a dress."

Dee's eyes narrowed. "But the whole point is to see if you can capture Maggie's essence better than she can herself."

"Dee."

Her eyes widened. "Pick a dress or I walk out that door. The mountains are calling."

She paled. I had never threatened before to leave the set. I could tell from the quick flicker in her face that she realized that, too.

"Calm down. What is it that you think captures your bride?"

"English."

"Okay, do you think the perfect dress for her is sexy? Modern? Fashionable? Lacey?"

"Pick one."

"JT, help me out. You know her better than I do."

This talk did not help my headache. "Traditional elegant."

Dee sorted through the dresses. She stopped at one dress that was off-white, silk, simple, and floor length. "What do you think?"

"Perfect."

CHAPTER 11

Maggie

THE SHOW ELVES arrived with JT's choice. The cameras were glued on me as I waited for the first sight of the dress. A young girl with a blonde ponytail rounded the corner carrying the plainest dress I have ever seen dotted with lace. If I were prone to be ultra conservative, I wouldn't even pick it. It was off-white. The color worked with my blonde hair, but other than that, it was plain.

"Time for you to put it on," the assistant said. "Then we'll do the big reveal to see if it's the dress or not."

"Good grief. Someone has been watching too many of those reality shows."

"Hurry. We're behind on the shooting."

I grabbed the weak dress from the assistant and slipped it on. I glanced in the mirror. The dress showcased my body well. Had to give JT that, but as I twisted and turned

169

in front of the mirror, my heart sank. I felt like Old Mother Hubbard. Not giving me time to think about it, the assistant rushed me out to the stage they had set up for my big debut. I stood on it and twisted and turned.

JT dashed over to me. "That's stunning."

I choked back words and did several more spins for the camera before I was instructed to slip into my own pick. My chest tightened, not sure how JT would handle red for a wedding gown.

It didn't take me long to slip into it. The fabric was silk. The cold texture awakened my senses.

I looked in the mirror. The red brought out my eyes, my white skin, and contrasted well with the blonde in my hair. The cut slipped over the curves of my body, emphasizing all the right places and playing down all the other spots.

This was it. This was the dress.

A crew member hustled me out to the podium, where JT's gaze met mine. I gasped, waiting. He had the slightest frown before he caught himself and smiled at me.

He didn't like it.

I spun to show off all the sparkle.

"It doesn't have to be traditionally white," Pearl said.

A frown appeared on JT's face, and so went my hopes for the red dress. "I like the off-white better," I said, "It feels more like a wedding."

JT looked at me with relief. "It does, doesn't it?"

"It's boring," Pearl said. "You should be trail blazing, not conforming."

JT stepped up to Pearl, guarding her from coming close to me. "No, Maggie is right. Elegance is the best choice."

I looked at my man standing up for me because I had chosen what he liked. What would happen if I ever picked wrong? Would he stand up for me then? What would he think of our relationship if he knew I was much more a red wedding gown, make a splash gal?

* * *

JT

After picking the dress, we had time off to grab a lunch —ham sandwiches, green salads, and chips from the craft table before strolling over to a New Age store called The Mystic Journey where Maggie and I would pick some rocks.

"Why picking rocks?" I asked Dee even though I had already agreed to go along with it with Maggie.

"Stress release." Dee pushed her large black sunglasses onto her head.

"For true stress release, take me to the mountains to hike with no camera. I want time to think about my upcoming marriage without the whole world watching. I did this additional show because you said it would make Maggie happy. You were lying to me about that."

"I did not—"

"Or you were wrong. Either way I didn't want to do this. So be glad I am going along with it."

Maggie jogged up behind me and seized my hand as we jaywalked across the street to the store. A store with a name like The Mystic Journey couldn't be anything other than weird, but if it would calm Maggie and give interest to the show, then we would go.

Once we walked inside, a bell chimed. Smells and scents assaulted me along with the array of tourist trap knickknacks laid out before us. The place overflowed with junk and fancy carvings from rocks, collections of dolls, books, jewelry, and statues. In the middle of the store, by the cashier, sat buckets of rocks. Dodging several tourists, I made it to the register. I dug my hands into a basket. The texture and coolness of the rocks reminded me of the earth. As I held them, Maggie came up close and touched my upper arm. She leaned around me.

"They're supposed to have a special powers."

Without saying a word, I eyed the price tag—they were only a couple of dollars. "Want one?"

She laid one finger on her cheek, thinking. "How about we pick one for each other, depending on what we think the other person needs?"

"What?"

Maggie pointed at the back of the bin, explaining what that particular rock helped with.

"Hmm." Maggie was into some different things.

"Come on, it'll be fun."

I pressed my lips together. This was getting ridiculous. Out of the corner of my eye, I read the opalite rock's signage: *"Brings calm, and stabilizes hormones and moods."* Yes, please! I grabbed one of the shiny white rocks and handed it to her.

"This one's perfect for you."

She rolled it around in her hands.

"It's pretty." She stepped closer to read about it. A smirk spread across her face as she playfully hit my side. "Okay, game on." She studied the meaning of various rocks. She strolled in front of the bins and around to the rocks on the other side before making her selection.

"I found the perfect one." She picked up a bluish-black round rock and dropped it into my hand. *"Cobalt Aura Quartz,"* its sign read. *"Good for alleviating restlessness and discontentment, plus enhanced natural clairvoyance, which leads to joy."*

That didn't sound bad.

I grabbed the rocks and went to pay for them with the cameras following me for effect. Maggie joined me and looked at the clerk. "Do these rocks really help with the aspects listed on their signs?"

The dark-haired teenage boy glanced up. "They can be powerful. If you keep one with you all day, really cool things happen."

Maggie snatched the bag from the store clerk's hand and held it close to her heart as though absorbing the rock energy. Did she believe in this stuff? She couldn't, could she?

* * *

NEXT, Dee instructed us to walk to another store, but wouldn't tell us what it was. That made me extremely suspicious. My neck itched thinking about what she could possibly be trying to pull over on us. We followed the producer without saying a word in the afternoon light. The temperature was a perfect seventy-three degrees and the air crystal clear.

The entire crew followed Maggie and me into a murky shop with dark rugs hanging on the wall, statues of elephant gods on the counters, and lit incense filling up the dark place.

"Wow." Maggie dropped my hand to look at the elephant people. "Don't you just love this stuff?"

Did she expect me to answer? She looked at me waiting, so I guess she did. "It is certainly unique." My grandmother used that old trick when she didn't approve of something.

Maggie agreed. "It is. This is so cool. I hope we are seeing a healer. That would be so fun."

"A healer?"

"A person with a special gift of being able to see your energy and who can heal it if it needs it."

I glanced at my watch. I guessed healers weren't conscious of being on time for the shooting schedule. I wandered over to a pile of books in the corner. One was on witchcraft and another on herbs. It was time to go if you asked me.

Before I could think of a way out of this, a petite lady with pure white hair and a big grin hobbled into the front room. "Welcome." Her voice was deep and cracked, supposedly with wisdom of time. "I'm so glad you're here. Please remove your shoes and leave them at the front door. Part of the healing process begins now, and we need you both to be grounded with the earth."

I wrestled with my shoes until Maggie pointed over to a simple wooden chair and told me to sit. I did what she instructed. She sank down to the hardwood floor on bended knee and removed my tennis shoe. Production could do all sorts of things with that shot.

"First thing we're going to do is to have you go to our

tandem room, and each have your chakras cleared. Do you know what chakras are?"

Maggie raised her hand like she was an excited schoolgirl. "They're energy centers we have in our body."

The lady nodded. "Correct. Sometimes the different chakras become blocked or aren't working as well as they should. We're going to clear them up today."

"Good job," I whispered to Maggie.

"Thanks," she said. "You meet a lot of New Agers in California."

The tightness in my chest eased from that comment. She had a reason for knowing all this. It didn't mean she was going to start talking to spirit guides and transform our home into a shrine for the elephant people.

A few minutes later, I found myself lying on a table next to Maggie. The room was full of windows. Light seeped through the fabric curtains hung over the windows to provide privacy. We both had our clothes on, to my great relief.

The white-haired lady lowered my table closer to the ground as a young blond gentleman waved his hands over Maggie. The tight muscles in her body relaxed into the mattress. Soft New Age music played in the background, and the lights dimmed except for the bright sunlight that slipped through the curtain cracks.

The older lady waved her arms in circles over my torso. She'd stop to feel something in the air above me, and waved again. A look of concentration appeared on her face like she needed to think about my stomach.

My gut tightened reflectively. No one has ever paid that much attention to that part of my body before. I reached out and took Maggie's hand into mine. The warmth of her fingers sunk into me.

The supposed healer continued in silence, nose wrinkled, hovering over my gut. "You're blocked in the first and fourth chakra." She waved her hands over me some more as though the air had answers. "You're not feeling grounded. You are guarded."

I said nothing to that. That was ridiculous. More of Dee's ploys to get a response for her stupid show.

"Guarding from what?" Maggie dropped my hand. She lay on the table next to me. A note of panic rang in her voice.

This was ridiculous. "They're only creating drama for the show, Maggie." The lady kept waving her fingers and touching me every now and then.

I closed my eyes and was near sleep when Maggie asked, "You still want to get married, don't you?"

"You're putting too much stock in this stuff. We're fine. Don't let this lady stir up trouble."

"Your throat chakra is closed off," the man said to her.

Nonsense. Nonsense. Nonsense. "Maggie's throat isn't closed off, and I'm not guarded," I snapped. The second after I said it, I wished I hadn't. I was starting to lose my professional grip.

Maggie seemed satisfied with my response about the chakra comment, and the lull of the silence enticed me into a deep sleep. I woke a few times to the lady touching me. She mostly waved her arms over my chest and legs. She said something about sending positive waves to aid my healing. I woke to her tapping the bottom of my foot.

"Thank you. Take your time getting up."

I stretched. An afternoon nap was what I needed, even if it meant being poked every now and then. Maggie looked like she had fallen asleep, too. When she opened her eyes, she smiled at me with a guilty grin and stood. I wrapped my arms around her. "That was a nice surprise."

Maggie smiled at me. "Well, at least you had a nap, and I know before marriage that I'm marrying a snorer."

I denied being a snorer and took Maggie by the hand.

She started talking to the lady who waved her hands above me. "How can we boost our chakra energies?"

That subject needed to be stopped.

"Well—" the lady started to say.

I tugged on Maggie's hand. "We have a schedule to meet."

"I'll come back." She waved to the lady.

We plunged out of the building right into Dee who, if I wasn't mistaken, wore cleaner clothes and looked more put together. I pulled back, blinked into the camera, and said to the soon-to-be audience, "Whenever Dee shows up, you know it's not good."

Dee smiled at us. "Big news. All the A-list actors want to come to your wedding. There are some seriously big names."

Maggie's grip on my hand lessened.

"I can't say who they are other than you know them. The whole world knows them. Because so many want to come, production has agreed to move your wedding out of Sedona to LA."

She clapped her hands together. "Isn't that so amazing? It's going to be a red-carpet affair. With some of the biggest stars wishing you two happiness."

"More likely, wanting to grab more airtime."

Ignoring me, Dee directed her attention to Maggie. "We have huge decisions to make, such as who'll be your brides-maids, and what type of bachelorette party you want to throw. It'll say a lot about which stars you pick. Since we're going to LA, the options are limitless."

"We aren't moving the wedding to LA." I started back toward the hotel. "The contract didn't say I had to do that. I could care less what some overpaid movie actors want."

I looked back, Maggie right behind me, and Dee jogging just in front of the camera crew. Dee blinked at me as though hearing me for the first time. "But the actors and Hollywood... Maggie?"

I stopped walking to see how my fiancée would handle this. She was baiting Maggie. Both of our gazes zeroed-in on Maggie.

She paled as her head swiveled from one of us to the other. "In LA, Olivia could come, and it would be nice to make the actors happy if they really want to come, but we have already planned everything here. We'd have to re-plan everything again. Plus, finding the right spot available on short notice in LA might be hard. The show doesn't have as much clout in LA as it does here. If we shoot in Sedona it is closer to JT's world, and I think the audience is more expecting that."

I stared at her. She had proceeded to say a whole lot of nothing. She was trying to please all of us—Olivia, me, and Dee, and by doing that she didn't take a side.

"But what do *you* want?" I fixed my gaze on her, but she didn't return it.

Instead, she flushed. "Our audience is used to JT liking

nature and seeing him in that kind of setting. If staying makes him happy, let's keep him happy."

She had stuck by my side instead of choosing Hollywood. She really was a team player.

Dee jumped in before Maggie could say anything more. "I could see which movie stars will be willing to come here."

My grasp tightened on Maggie's hand. We had just won this round. Maggie had been right about waiting to fight for what mattered. She had been right to foresee that something was coming and rock picking wasn't that big of an issue.

"It's a destination point for the stars," Dee continued. "I could make it more exclusive and a bigger deal." She looked up as though thinking about it. "Yeah, I could make that work."

The spin-doctor was at her best.

"Maggie," Dee continued, "I don't mean this in any way offensive, but since you're going to be hanging out with some of the most beautiful women in the world, we're going to need to take your appearance up to top-notch."

I stepped up in front of Maggie to protect her from this witch. "I like my fiancée the way she is."

Dee leaned around me to look at Maggie as though I hadn't said anything. "At first glimpse, we want the audience's breath taken away."

Maggie let go of my hand and touched my arm gently as she leaned around me. "But aren't you guys shooting right now? Can't the audience see me already looking plain?"

Neither woman was taking my comment into consideration. It was like I had suddenly become invisible.

"The viewers of this show will be nothing like what we expect for your big wedding. The event will appeal to a wider audience. Maggie, you'll have full star treatment. In just a few minutes, both of you are going to meet your new fitness trainer and dietitian to whip you two into shape. After you are done with him, we are spray-tan the both of you."

"Are not," I said.

"Am," Dee said.

I stepped up closer to Dee. "We're not going on national television with orange skin. If you try to push me on this or Maggie, you will fail in court. You don't have the right to compromise our health. That's not in the contract."

"I don't want to look orange, either." Maggie came up behind me.

We joined hands, taking on Dee with a united front.

Dee's eyes narrowed. "Fine. I'll cancel the tan if you don't fight me on the trainer and the food." She pitched it like this was a business negotiation, which I guess it was. She was trying to make a show, and I was trying to hold onto a sense of normalcy.

From her solid stance and set jaw, it was clear we might fight rounds for an awfully long time. This lady had endurance and grit not to lose.

"Fine."

CHAPTER 12

ℳaggie

JT's EYES held panic when the shop owner told him he wasn't "grounded." Panic. I had never seen that before. What would cause such a reaction? He squeezed my hand, bringing my attention back to him as we soared up to our room on our triumphant elevator ride.

He punched the button for the fifth floor and, as the doors closed and we started moving, I cast him a little sideways look. "We did good."

He grinned. "We're a good team."

I smiled up at him. "You're a good negotiator." I blew kisses at him.

He laughed. "Especially when someone's trying to make us orange."

"No orange for us."

"Nope," he agreed.

"Do you always get what you want?" I asked.

He leaned a shoulder against the elevator, still holding onto my hand. "Almost always. Why? Do you want something? Want me to take on Dee for you, again? Diamonds on your dress? A new chakra rock?"

I laughed and pressed up against his hard body, feeling safe and happy, yet faintly uneasy. The way JT had dealt with Dee felt a lot like the way he dealt with me sometimes. Like he was always working a deal.

Once our elevator arrived, JT left to change with no parting words or kiss. While I tried to recover from my disappointment, I found Dee waiting for me in my hotel room. "Let's go." She clapped her hands together.

My eyes narrowed. "How did you get here so fast?"

"Ran up the stairs."

"Of course." I sighed. Why was Dee suddenly on such a health kick? She was acting... different. "Let me get into my gym clothes." I opened my hotel room door and strolled to my suitcase to find my shorts and a T-shirt.

Despite Dee's push to rush, I wasn't feeling a need to hurry. Lifting weights sounded dreadful, and I hadn't done something like that in years. Plus, I knew the end result wouldn't be muscles or a slender body because three days wasn't enough. All I would achieve from this event would be aches, and embarrassment when the episode aired.

Dee kicked her foot back up on the wall as she leaned against it. "Are you worried about JT?"

My focus snapped on her. "What? Why would I be?"

She shrugged. "I don't know. I would be if a healer just told me my fiancé's heart was closed."

She was baiting me again. Damn, she was good. "The

healer said he wasn't grounded, and that makes sense. We were doing all this shopping, stuff not in his element. I'd be the same way if we were riding horses all day and petting snakes."

Dee laughed. "Now there's an idea."

I waved my finger at her. "Don't you dare. I'll come after you with vengeance if you get me anywhere close to more animals."

She laughed harder. "It isn't the grounded part that would worry me with JT, it's the closed heart part."

I snatched my old blue T-shirt and headed toward the bathroom to change and to brush off that statement. Dee wasn't going to succeed in planting any more doubt. "You put her up to it."

I tugged on the old clothes. The longer we shot the less I cared how I looked. I guess that was what lack of sleep would do for a person. That, and cause more impatience with Dee.

"Did no such thing," Dee called to me. "You can see it if you think about it. He hasn't been talkative lately, and he kind of sits back and lets us run the whole show. He was never like that before."

"That doesn't mean anything," I snapped as I returned to the bedroom.

Dee shrugged, but gave me this concerned looked. "I hope not." She let out a puff of air. "We're really counting on a wedding."

She let that statement drop, then busied herself with the walkie-talkie, making sure JT was en route as we made it to the workout room. The makeup artist immediately scurried around me.

JT stumbled into the weight room, looking tired with black lines under his eyes and shoulders slumped.

Maybe Dee was right. He didn't look happy.

I stood on my tiptoes and kissed his cheek. "Baby, you ready to work out?"

He leaned into my touch.

"Okay, okay," came a loud male voice. "Break up the romance. This is a competition; we can't have anyone getting mushy here. We're at the hard-core ab bootcamp." The voice was deep and rough, sounding like the owner was a big muscly man ready to rip us to shreds. Instead, there stood a short, wiry, blond boy.

Giving JT a wobble of the head, I clapped my hands together. "I'm ready. How many sit ups are we doing?"

JT laughed at my antics.

The trainer gave a hint of a smile and slapped a twenty-pound barbell in JT's palm. "Love the attitude from the lady."

"She is something," JT said.

I slapped the other dumbbell into JT's other hand. "Glad you think so." I winked at my man.

"Abs in," yelled the trainer.

I about-faced and sucked in my gut.

"To your back," came the next order. "Tight abs protect your whole body."

I sucked in, and the trainer strolled in front of me, examining me, hunting for defects. He tapped me on the top of my head.

"Grow taller," he commanded, handing me three-pound dumbbells.

That made no sense, but I straightened up my back as high as I could.

"Good. Arm curls!" yelled the trainer.

I pumped, but there was no way I could keep up with JT's arm curls. It was like he was on the racetrack lapping me. He swung his arms, accentuating muscles on his biceps and making beads of sweat form on his forehead. I found it incredibly sexy.

"Zoom in on my man," I yelled. "He's looking mighty fine."

JT flushed, like he was embarrassed.

Immediately, the wiry Mr. Muscles had me dive into a very long round of squats. My thighs were on fire, my knees refusing to bend, and my lower back throbbing. My efforts probably looked more like a stumble than a squat.

Muscle man's voice boomed louder in my ear. "Hundred percent commitment, yeah? Straighten your back. Hold your head higher. Tummy in. Go deeper."

"I need to be able to move for the rest of the show and for my wedding," I complained as sweat streamed down the sides of my face.

"Yeah, we have to be able to move," JT chimed in.

I looked over at him and he winked. We were in this together. Hating it. I almost laughed. It was good to be aligned with JT.

He stood from his squat. "Well, that was fun. Now we're done."

I blew out a sigh of relief and limped over to the water cooler.

"But we still have twenty minutes," the trainer declared.

"Nope." JT used a hand towel to wipe at his forehead. "You got enough. Now we're going for ice cream."

What a great negotiator. I hobbled over to him.

Dee bustled into the room. "Next is waxing, tanning, and a couple of other things."

JT and I looked at each other. His eyebrows arched ever so lightly.

So did mine.

He grabbed my hand, and we ran away from Dee, the waxes, the tanning, and the pressures of trying to perform for so many people—including each other. We ran for ice cream together, though we didn't quite shake the camera crew.

* * *

JT

My blood pumped heartily through my body. I glanced at Maggie, whose hand I held as we sprinted down the street hunting for an ice cream parlor. We needed to escape this pressure cooker we had volunteered for.

"You okay?" Maggie asked tentatively, a bit out of breath.

"I am not doing the tanning or waxing. You can if you want."

She shook her head as she struggled to keep up with me. "No, no."

She was being a good sport with our jail break. Of course, she had escaped before. I was beginning to understand. Maybe she wasn't as flakey as I had thought. Maybe I had been too hard on her.

"You are stunning in your wedding gown. It made everything seem so real seeing you standing there looking like my bride."

Instead of smiling or seeming pleased like I expected, she stiffened. "Dee and I have a surprise for you."

I took a step back. "What?" Despite my efforts, my voice sounded strained.

"Well, you know how Dee mentioned vortexes?"

"Yes?"

"Dee and I thought for our grand entrance to the ceremony, we'd take a hot air balloon to the top of a mountain where the vortex is the strongest, and then land with violins playing punk classical on the mountainside."

She must have had her punch spiked by that nasty Dee, who was in it all for the drama of the show and the ratings. So, despite the fact that I knew the cameras were on me wanting to capture my expression, and that I was used to controlling my reactions from being on the TV show before. Despite the fact that I loved the woman, I lost my cool.

"Are you out of your mind?" I asked. "We aren't doing that."

"Why not?" Maggie put her hands on her hips. "It's an adventure. No one else I know of has ever done it."

What was she saying? Since when did it matter what other people were doing?

"Sounds dangerous. Besides, a vortex is a concept that someone made up so they could drive tourists to this town."

Dee strode through the camera people trailing us. "We're going to test that theory out right now. Everyone in their cars. JT and Maggie, the cameras will shoot you two traveling together to the vortex. You two will climb the mountain to absolutely the most stunning view you've ever seen. Somewhere along the way on the trip to the vortex, I want you talking about the vortex. What you believe about it.

"Say what you want. I'd like you to voice your real opinions but, for show purposes, it'd be best if you two had different opinions. You two bounce them back and forth with each other and then resolve your differences at the top of the vortex mountain with what is going to be one of your most famous kisses."

She slapped her hands together. "Okay, everyone has their marching orders. Let's get going."

I stopped walking. "We're going for ice cream." I moved closer and looked down on Dee to remind her she was much shorter than me.

"After the vortex." She stood in front of me hands on her hips. "We have light considerations. We need to shoot the outdoor stuff while the sun is up. We can shoot the ice cream after or… tell you what, you and Maggie can do the ice cream thing without the cameras or do whatever you want. Have the night off. How does that sound?"

There went Dee again wheeling and dealing. The deal was sound as long as I talked all parties out of the insane idea, which shouldn't be too hard to do. The only thing left to do was for me to figure out a deal Maggie would go for. "Fine." I squeezed my fiancée's hand. "You up for a hike later? The mountains are calling us."

She burst in a large grin. "We're really going to the vortex right now? I'm so excited."

* * *

TWENTY MINUTES LATER, my eyes fastened on the largest mountain range west of the hotel. "Sweetheart, all this wedding stuff is stressful. We should rent a CJ7 Jeep and explore those mountains over there."

"Oh-h-kay?" Maggie said.

There was something odd in her voice. She stared out the window in the opposite direction of the mountain. Maybe all this wedding stuff was getting to her as much as it was getting me. We needed to let go in nature. "My hunch is we'd see bobcats, mountain lions, and maybe an antelope. And hidden valleys, if we hike deep enough."

"Maybe," she muttered, still not looking at the mountain.

"You know there're similarities between the crystals stuff and the peace I find in nature. They're basically the same thing, so I think you'd love it."

She needed to relax. Be in nature. Let things go. I rolled down my window. A huge gust of wind slipped into the car, bringing with it rich smells of pine, sage, and fresh air. I took a deep breath, allowing all of it in.

Maggie cleared her throat.

I reached over and touched her arm. "Are you okay?"

She brushed at her hair. Her fingers fiddled with tangles. She patted my hand and glanced up at me. "Do you want to do our homework now or when we arrive?"

Homework? "I don't know."

She continued to brush at her windblown hair to keep it out of her mouth. "You have a problem doing our assignment?"

Oh, yeah. That. Dee required having us on camera having a disagreement about the vortexes. I was never going to say yes to one of these shows again. My eyes flicked back to the mountains. "I'd rather not argue at all. We're not faking a fight for the camera."

Beside me, Maggie shifted, like she was uncomfortable. But, when I finished, she turned to me with a decisive nod. "I agree," she said. "I don't want to fake arguments either. Dee is becoming panicky that there isn't enough drama for the show."

Good. We were on the same page and thinking alike. That gave us negotiating power.

I squinted my brows. "What are vortexes, anyway?"

Maggie turned toward me, her shoulders back, her face bright. She leaned toward me in her excitement, the seatbelt strained against her chest. "They're places around the world where there's extra energy. You've seen water spinning or wind? Well, people believe that is an energy that's supposed to be amazingly healing. Sedona has many vortex sites. That's why it's so famous."

My hands encircled the steering wheel more tightly. "You've got to be kidding. I have to tell you, Mags, that sounds more like good marketing than good energy."

Her face fell, and she shook her head. "No, really, I've heard about it for years in California."

"Ah. Well, if you heard about it in *California*," I mumbled.

I thought about Maggie and her enthusiasm for things. For life. Her energy. "I bet your hair lifts on its ends in a vortex," I said thoughtfully.

She laughed. "Okay, and you?"

"My hair stays flat, even in high humidity."

She batted my arm. "No, how do you think you'd respond?"

"No, clue. Are you seriously asking me how I will react to unseen energy?

Maggie nodded. "I am."

Next, she'd tell me these were spots where aliens visited. "How do they determine what spots have this 'power?'"

She shifted away from me to face forward. She crossed her arms. "Some people believe this is where aliens visit Earth."

I chuckled. "This sounds like a complete waste of an afternoon that we could have spent alone together exploring the mountains." Those mountains had taken on a rusty hue.

Maggie wasn't laughing. Her shoulders slumped before she cleared her throat.

I glanced at her. Vortexes. "Okay, tell me more about this alien-attracting vortex we're headed to. Oh, hey, look!" My voice rose as I pointed out the windshield to a hawk soaring overhead.

Maggie sat straight up. "What? What? We're getting close to the vortex; do you see something cool?"

"Yes." I crunched down in my seat to keep my finger aimed at the hawk. "See him?"

"Him? Him, who?"

"The hawk! I think it was red-tailed."

She stared at me, then lowered herself back to her seat, smiling a little. "You really do love to be out in nature, don't you?"

I blew out a breath. "I need it. And I haven't gone for... way too long. What with the show, and then work, and..."

"Me," she said softly.

I reached out and squeezed her hand. "No, not you. Just life."

Her hand was petite, but strong, in mine as she squeezed it tightly. "Don't worry. If that's what you need, we'll get it for you."

I glanced over. She looked... serene. And content.

"You'd love it too, Maggie," I said, eager to share. "It'll have the same effect on you as those rocks. Better, in fact. I know it." I was confident. Certain I could make her love the things I loved. She only had to experience it for herself. "We'll go camping as soon as this crazy wedding is out of the way."

"Out of the..." she repeated the words softly, then it was her turn to point excitedly out the window. "Oh, oh, there it is! One of the hottest spots for the vortex, and where I want us to exchange our vows."

It turned out to be a happening place with parking spots in high demand. Cars lined up the hill and circled the lot.

Maggie willed a spot to open up. "Open, open, open," and a space opened.

The sun spread orange on the land. I slipped out of the car and paused to take it in.

Maggie headed toward the foot of the mountain path. "Over here," she called.

Fresh air refreshed my lungs as I gazed up at the intense royal-blue sky scattered with strings of white clouds.

Another masterpiece for nature's constantly shifting displays.

"This is great, Mags, I'm glad we're here together. I needed this time with you."

Maggie bounced on the tips of her toes like a kid at Disneyland. "I'm so glad." Beyond her, cameramen scoured up the path, their lenses already locked in on us. "Isn't this stunning?" her voice was muted by the hum of cars driving by.

"Where would people park for the wedding? There're only a few spots."

She pressed her lips into a line as she gave that thought. "Maybe they'd have to bus everyone in." She grabbed hold of the guardrail, hoisting herself up the hill. "Do you feel anything?"

I hurried after her, my breath already increasing with the mountain's rapid incline. "No." The heat of the day lowered as the sun continued to fade downward in the sky. The cooler temperature only sped up Maggie's chatter. She walked far ahead of me and talked too fast for me to grasp most of what she said, but at least we were outside.

As we climbed, the air thinned, and the rock changed to more rust and tannish colors mixed with earth shades of reds and dark oranges. A gentle breeze swept in and kissed my cheeks until we had reached the crest. Maggie had arrived before me and walked around as if on a tightrope to take in the view.

"I'm sooo dizzy."

She took tiny steps toward me. She closed her eyes. "Ooh, do you feel that? A huge vibration is zipping up my right leg and up my right side. Nothing is going up my left leg." Her eyes opened. "Is it the same for you? Close your eyes and try it."

"No."

She squinted at me. "What?"

"I don't feel anything, and I don't want to close my eyes. I'll keep a lookout, you... feel things."

People brushed past her. They gathered by the edge of the mound overlooking Oak Creek Canyon, sometimes called the Grand Canyon of Sedona, with its deep ravine and giant, thunderous mountains beyond. I hopped from the mound of rock we stood on over to a nearby jetting rock on the mountainside.

A stunning sight of the deep ravine spread out for miles with red and green mixing together as the shadows played games on the rocks, scrubby trees, and scrub brush. Beyond rose those red rock mountains. The wind sung by my ears in small bursts of energy.

Well. Maybe I did believe in vortexes.

Maggie signaled for me to come to her with energetic waving arms. She was missing all the wonder of nature and was determined to have me miss it, too. I scurried up to her and whispered in her cute ear, "Stunning, isn't it?"

Her fingers circled around my shirt sleeve. "Are you feeling anything?"

She cast those large eyes on me, causing me to find this silliness as somehow charming. She gripped my shirt sleeve tighter.

"My head instantly felt the pressure since we came up here. You don't feel it?" She closed her eyes. "I'm dizzy." The sun spilled its last ray around her, making her glow angelically.

I reached out to steady her.

She opened her eyes. "Don't you feel that? My stomach's fluttering. A vibrating tingle is going up my right side." She squirmed. "It's so weird." Her hands grasped her stomach. "I don't feel so well." She took a deep cleansing breath. "How do you feel?"

All my attention was on her. I had to give some thought to how I felt. "I... feel nothing but what I normally do—a deep appreciation for being in nature."

She looked at me with wide eyes like my response surprised her.

Maggie was being so... so... well, I wasn't sure what. Maybe "alive" was the word for it? Or "open?" Or "free" to experience whatever came her way?

A knot formed in the base of my skull. I stretched my neck side to side and took a deep, broad, centering breath.

The problem with being "free" and "open..." It caused you to experience a whole lot of pain. Like right now, Maggie was feeling high emotion... and a tingle that made her sick, but excited.

When I let myself be open and felt that kind of emotion, I'd been crushed. Sickened. Guilty as hell.

Experiencing emotions wasn't my job. Protecting Maggie was my job. Getting stuff done was my job.

And, right now, Maggie was about to need someone to carry her down the mountain, despite the fact we had a lot of stuff to get done. Such as changing the I-have-so-many-feelings vortex wedding to something more reasonable.

I loved her free nature, but I was never going to be like that. I couldn't. Still, because *she* was, it drew me to her. I wanted to absorb that lightness. It brought such happiness with it.

Before could give all this more thought, Dee joined us.

"So, what do you think?" the producer gestured to the whole setting. "This is where Maggie wants to ride a hot air balloon. You'd land over here." She strolled to the flattest rock surface of the area. "You'd be decked out in your wedding gear. We could have you each arrive on the same balloon or in separate ones."

I eyed the rough terrain. They couldn't be serious. Were they setting me up to get a good scene for the show? I laughed. "You two are *really* funny. There's no flat surface, it isn't legal, and the airport is too close."

Maggie grabbed up higher on my sleeve. "Wow, that energy is going to the other side of my body. This is a rush. I'm so dizzy."

I grabbed both her arms and helped her over to the guard rail. It was time for us to leave before I ended up carrying her down the mountain. This was definitely a no-go for an actual ceremony.

As we head back to sturdier ground, the cameras moved along on both sides of us, and Dee followed us with a smirk on her face. She'd definitely use this: Maggie "feeling the energy" and me saying no.

The muscles in my back tightened like when I'd hiked the last bit of a steep mountainside. I followed Maggie, keeping my arms out in case she fell. Of course, I wasn't saying a lot. These were crazy ideas.

Reckless, over-the-top, *fun* ideas.

But crazy.

We stopped at the top of the mound. Maggie took a

deep breath. "Oh, it's gone." She closed her eyes to double-check and then opened them. "That was a rush. Whew. You guys feel it?"

No one said a word, probably hoping I would. Maggie had proven she was highly suggestible. No fortune tellers for her. She seized my shirt right under my chest and pulled herself tighter to me. I wrapped my arm around her thin waist as a rose scent from her hair tickled my nose. "You okay?"

She smiled. "This would be an awesome place to have a wedding, wouldn't it? I've never heard of a wedding with a hot air balloon. That would be a total rush."

"Let's see... unpredictable wind, no flat surfaces, less than a thousand feet before toppling into a deep canyon, and vortex energy that makes you sick and dizzy. What wouldn't I love about the idea?"

Acting like she didn't hear me, Maggie muttered, "You'd never forget our wedding."

CHAPTER 13

M aggie

THE SPINNING and swirling on my right side had died down to a reverberation once I stepped out of the direct line of the energy pocket.

"Did you feel something?" I stepped up to Dee at the base of the mountain.

She shrugged. "I think so."

"Do you think this energy helps people stay young?"

"I read it did." She glanced at her clipboard, probably checking what was next on the schedule.

"I wanted to explore it more, but JT bee-lined off the mountain. I thought you said he'd love it."

Dee looked up from her clipboard. "Ask him what's going on."

I pursed my lips. I knew not to trust Dee. She always had an angle, but that advice actually sounded wise.

A few minutes later, we were in the car with just me, him, and the cameras. I didn't say anything until he started driving. I reached over and rubbed his taut neck as he propelled the vehicle into the darkening day. "Relax, baby," I purred into his ear.

He half chuckled before leaning into my hands. "That feels good." Letting his reaction encourage me, I kissed his cheek and whispered, "The good news is, we're going to get married!"

He shook his head like I was silly, which I guess I was. He seemed to like it, though. "Yes, we are."

My stomach eased. Maybe I was making things up about why he was being quiet. Maybe I should take him at his word. We'd gone through the rounds on that before.

"Dee wants us to clean up and then meet her at the coffee shop down from our hotel."

His shoulders stiffened. "Can't we call it a night? She said we could have it off. The plan was ice cream or the mountains."

I sat back in my car seat, my head hurting. And people said women were moody. "Apparently not. And, we've already been to the mountains."

JT slowed the car as dust billowed behind us. "I'm not okay with doing stupid things that could have us both injured or worse, and I'm not hip on magical spots of energy."

My shoulders slumped with his words and I found myself not having anything more to say.

The sun had faded as we pulled up to a dim-lit coffee shop and climbed out of the car. The blackness of the night wrapped around the town. JT had sprayed himself with cologne at the hotel. The rustic smell lured me to come closer, but I resisted. It would be easy to lean into his body and into his opinions.

Maybe too easy.

"Are you coming?" He held out a hand to enter the coffee shop with him.

From the corner of my eye, I caught a glimpse of the light on the cameras. No time for emotional reactions for all the world to see. So much happened today, from the energy rocks to the awful dress, that made me feel yucky. And, JT kept giving me looks like he thought I was slightly off.

Maybe I was. Maybe it was smart to just go with the flow.

Dee gestured at us.

"Here's the deal," Dee said once we sat at a coffee table. "We only have a week, and we have to agree tonight where we're going to have the actual wedding. So many other choices are dependent on it, and arrangements need to be made."

I held my breath as she spoke, not daring to glance at JT. This was a big decision.

"Because of JT's objections and Maggie's negative reaction to all the energy, the vortex mountain won't work. My scouts found a lovely valley that could work instead."

Dee had managed to insult both JT and me on national TV in one swoop. "That said, we'll use the valley."

"A valley?" JT sounded like he expected some twist that would make it awful.

The valley sounded like a good option to me.

I thought about JT, about all the changes he was making

just by coming here. How he'd done it for me... even if I didn't want it. About how hard this all was for him. Way harder than for me. I loved this kind of thing. JT hated it.

If I'd had a hard day, his must have been hell.

"Only if we have horses," I said loudly.

Dee and JT both turned to me with mouths gaping.

"What?" Dee's eyes showed white around her dark irises.

I sat up straight in my chair. "After we say 'I do' and exchange rings, then we climb on a horse and ride away into the sunset."

"Perfect!" Dee said.

"No horses," JT said.

It was my turn to stare. "Why not?"

JT looked away from me, pink coloring his neck.

Dee cleared her throat. "We'll keep that in for the consideration department. Now, let's explore what thoughts you two are having about the honeymoon." She raised her eyes slowly in a suggestive gesture.

"You're not filming that!" JT's hand hit the table. "I draw the line there. No way." He shifted in his seat. "And Maggie, you better not say to me you think it's a good idea or..."

A huge lump rose in my throat. I was doing all these things like cooking and picking a conservative wedding dress for him. I might be trying harder than he was. We had a huge chasm of differences to cross to make this marriage work. If only one of us was building bridges across it, it wouldn't work.

I forced myself to smile serenely. "I was never going to agree to that. Calm down, cowboy." I sounded more snappy than I meant it.

Dee held up her hands. "We want the American public to imagine your honeymoon. Their imagination is going to be much better than the reality."

Both JT and I scowled at her.

"America wants to get to know you as a couple."

JT leaned in toward the table. "If America hasn't figured it out yet, we're a very boring couple. That's not likely to change anytime soon. Show or no show."

"Break." Dee gestured toward the cameramen. "Let's take twenty."

The men scurried out of the shop with Dee, leaving me and JT alone, except for the shop owner, who wiped the front counter. Silence hung heavy between JT and me.

"So," I said brightly. "Where do you want to go on a honeymoon?"

JT wiped his brow. "Can't we stay here in Sedona? There's so much to discover." He reached for my hands. "How about going on a camping trip? We could hike every path here. That way, we can immerse ourselves in this beautiful land." He thought a second then added, "and we can go to the spa in between hikes."

I could almost feel the dust in my throat, threatening to choke me. The flies swarming around my eyes, landing on my arms, making my skin crawl from the germs spreading onto me. Not to mention the hard ground that, with each step, would pound my back.

"How long would you want to do that?" I asked tentatively, keeping my voice light, like whatever answer he gave would be fine.

He thought for a second before saying, "I've been

working nonstop for years. I've earned a break. I don't know, at least a month or two."

"A month or two!" The idea crowded my mind. It was hard to think clearly. "Wow. That's… long. My back has never really been the same from camping in your front yard, despite the multitude of chiropractic appointments. How do you think it would be if I slept on the ground for much longer than that?"

"We'll bring an air mattress, piles of foam, and tons of blankets. You'll be so comfortable. You'll never want to sleep anywhere else. Sweetheart, this could be what we need."

"What about work? Dimitri wouldn't like it."

He thought about that. "Fine, a week."

My head pounded. "For our honeymoon?" I couldn't keep out of my voice the desperation gnawing at me.

"Yes." He gave me his brilliant smile. "Being in nature has a way of peeling off stress. It's almost like you become one with it."

The honeymoon was supposed to be a wonderful celebration of our lives together, not him chasing his subconscious dream of becoming a mountain man.

* * *

TARZAN DREAMS PLAGUED me through the night. Would I have to become Jane to keep my man? The idea of camping for a week caused me to wake up in a hot sweat. No amount of makeup would hide my swollen eyes. There were large and puffy and ready to make the statement to the world that, yes, things weren't all blissful in the reality TV wedding world.

Why the heck did they call it "reality" TV? It was anything but. Still stewing on that, I showed up for a mindful organic breakfast, where we were to eat in silence. Dee's idea for the next episode of our show was JT and I spending a day of relaxation, which meant taking a trip with people on a silence retreat. Ugh.

Dee thought it would amuse the viewers watching me try to remain silent. I certainly didn't find it amusing. JT might appreciate the break, Dee had pointed out. I grunted when she said that. She might be right.

At breakfast there was no sign of JT, only Dee. I gathered my bowl of fruit and plopped down by her at a corner table.

"You look awful." She ignored the silence rule.

People looked at us as though we were sinning by talking.

"He wants to a week of camping for our honeymoon," I whispered to keep the glares down to the minimum.

"I heard." She took a crisp bite into her burnt toast. She chuckled. "Charming."

"I can't do that for a whole week."

She chewed on her toast. "Last time you didn't make it a night. But I'd love to shoot you trying." She gave me a wicked grin.

I glared at her, then stared at my fruit and all its bright colors. "I can't do it."

"Yes, you can. It will make JT happy, and you want to be his girl, right?"

"But camping?"

"You lost him last time by not doing it. But don't worry about that now. Today we're focusing on getting him out of his funk."

"How? All he wants to do is be outside."

"You two are going to Amitabha Stupa and Peace Park. It's a silent Buddhist outdoor park."

That sounded pretty amazing, except for the silent part. "JT might find that a bit weird."

"You said it yourself, nature calms him. We'll set his day off right, and turn this wedding funk around."

I was too miserable to question Dee. I'd seen JT return from a horse ride in much better spirits. Maybe Dee was right. She didn't want us to break up. That would ruin all her production plans, and I didn't want to break up because it would ruin my future, not to mention break my heart.

Twenty minutes later, armed with sun lotion, hot coffee, and a bright smile, I knocked on JT's hotel door. After a couple of minutes of waiting, I called out, "Hello?"

Nothing.

I pounded on the door. Twenty seconds later, it swung open. JT stood there in a towel wrapped around him and no other clothes. "Hi, beautiful."

The man could make me melt with two words. That was power. "Oh-h." I stepped back, then up to him, wrapping my arms around him. I buried my head against his bare damp chest.

He hooked one arm around me, the other hand still holding onto his towel. "What's the matter?"

"Nothing."

"Your eyes are puffy like you've been crying."

Perfect. He noticed. I held the sunscreen. "I come bearing gifts." I wiggled my eyebrows in a suggestive manner. "Let's get this on you."

A smile danced on the edge of his lips. He strolled to the corner of the bed and sat on it with small water droplets on his chest. I swallowed a lump in my throat before wiping a big streak of sun lotion across his rugged, strong chest. He leaned into my touch.

"You like me taking care of you," I whispered.

He grabbed my hand and pulled me to him for a kiss.

WE CLIMBED onto the bus and a big wall of noiselessness smacked us in the head. The bus brimmed with tourists in hats, sunglasses, and water bottles. No one said a word. One lady around my age with a sun-guard hat caught my eye, and I gave her a forced grin. She nodded in response. The silence was suffocating.

I led JT to the back seats, which were surprisingly still open. I scooted close to him and leaned my head on his shoulder. He eased into the silence like a comforting blanket. A few minutes later, short breathing noises slipped through his lips. As he relaxed into sleep, I stared out the window at the desert landscape listening to his jagged rhythm.

We hit a hard bump on the road, and the bus bounced from the motion. I reached out and stroked JT's arm, dancing my fingers through his dark thick arm hair. I did like being with him and would need to put up with that week in the mountains with tents so I wasn't away from him. I could do that more easily than be apart from him.

He woke a few minutes later, when the bus slowed at our destination. He whispered in my ear, "I like your touch."

His warm breath sent chills through me.

He grabbed my hand, and we hustled off the bus. He stopped to inhale the mountain air. I sighed and waited for him. The sun pressed on my face. I put my hand above my brow to shield my eyes, wishing I had on one of those sun protector hats worn by the other passengers. All of them had moved on into the park while we stood. I had a Thoreau on my hands... and expected the next thing he'd do would be mention a Walden Pond experience. Wait, he had done that in his own way with his idea about the honeymoon.

JT took a few steps, then stopped to absorb the atmosphere with all the patience of Gandhi. He did this several times. I fidgeted, trying to hide my impatience. The Buddhist Park spread over the hill in all directions.

I needed a break from the quiet or I would go mad.

CHAPTER 14

 T

BESIDES THE FACT that Buddhists like to worship a golden Buddha and didn't eat cows, I didn't know anything about them. I didn't even know if my assumptions formed a terrible stereotype, I should be ashamed about.

Remaining in silence offered me the opportunity to take in the stunning landscape of the ancient red rock mountains. They wore the history of the Earth in their structure. The soil had a faint rusty red that made the green vegetation pop. The sky maintained its deep blue, drawing me in.

The only noises came from different types of birds and the crunching sounds of footsteps on rocky dirt. Up ahead of us, scraps of fabric tied together with painted symbols flapped in the wind. The fabric pieces hooked together, creating a flag that traveled from one tree branch to another.

Maggie huffed and marched on ahead of me, giving me a wave goodbye. My stomach eased as I no longer felt her pressure to go faster. We were surely different. When Maggie wasn't happy about something, things didn't go to a low rumble like they had with Irene. I had already experienced Maggie's explosive nature and her intensity. That could become a concern.

Soon, I ran into white Buddha dolls about a foot-high placed under large trees with lots of smaller rocks laid around the figures. I drifted in an easy and trancelike state, reading prayers for peace. This was truly stunning land.

"Maybe we should move here," I whispered to Maggie when she slipped over to me.

"What?" she snapped, her eyes extremely wide. "Here?"

"We could find a nice house close to the mountains." Our shoes continued to crunch as we wandered around. "Wonder what a small house in Sedona would cost?" I thought out loud.

"Why here?" Maggie followed behind me on the dirt path.

"This is what I want." I stopped and took a full deep breath of the crystal clean air. "It wouldn't be as hot as Tucson. It would be a nice get-away for us."

"More wilderness," she muttered.

I smiled. "I know. Isn't it incredible?"

* * *

AT BREAKFAST THE NEXT DAY, I couldn't get the wild out of my head. Nature kept calling, and the wedding prep kept going on and on. It was super silly stuff about logistics, colors, and of course, dealing with the lawyer for the prenup... Maggie had signed it after I made sure she understood the terms, even though she refused to see how much money I had. The refusing to even want to know how much I had made my heart swell with affection. Proof we were *really* different... and that her way was good, too, and she was planning to stay with me.

I still tried to get some work done every day, but every time I pulled out files, Dee seemed to know and hunted me down to be in a scene. It gave me no space to work. No room to move. No quiet to think. Pressure built in my chest. I had to get away. If I was going to stand in front of the world and marry Maggie in two days, I had to ground myself.

After Maggie filled her plate up with eggs and fruits, she sat down next to me, looking as lovely as ever.

"Sleep well?" she asked.

"Tomorrow I'm taking off. I don't want you to worry."

She stared at me, her face growing pale. "Where?"

"The mountains."

"And you don't want me to go with you?"

"I need this, Maggie. You're going to be busy with the wedding. You'll have more fun here."

She didn't look too happy... a line crinkled her forehead. She was taking this harder than I expected. I kissed her quivering lips. "It's going to be okay." I needed her to understand. Or learn this about me. Or at least accept it.

Sometimes I had to get away in the wild alone. "Some men drink or cheat to cope. I escape to nature."

Her eyes narrowed. She was having none of this.

"Get together tonight with Dee and have a bachelorette party. Celebrate your last night of freedom."

Maggie's jaw dropped open.

I'd better explain. "I want you to have fun. You need a break. You and Dee seem like you could really have a good time together if you give it a chance."

"You want to leave me with Dee?"

"She's from California, too, and you have the show in common."

She blinked rapidly.

I kissed her quickly and whispered, "In two days we'll be husband and wife."

Her blue eyes stared at me. "I don't want to be with Dee."

"Then go to the spa and treat yourself to a shopping trip. Or whatever else you want to do. Have fun. I dug into my back-pants pocket and pulled out a credit card to hand her. She didn't take it.

"Don't leave me," she whispered.

* * *

THE AFTERNOON WAS a perfect temperature as I hustled to the outdoor-car rental place. Soon it would be me and the landscape. I ignored the camera crew following me until I ditched them.

An elderly man with a wild mane of gray hair greeted me at the rental counter. "Mountains calling you?"

I grinned. "Sure are."

"Let's get you hooked up."

After we completed the rental forms, I asked the man across the counter. "Where should I go?"

"Devil's Bridge if you're short on time."

Good enough. He pointed it out on the map and dove into detail. I shook my head to stop him. I wanted to explore with no previous knowledge of the place beforehand. He let out a crack of a smile as if he'd seen the likes of me many times before. "Ladies and Gentlemen, we have an explorer in our midst."

Seeing the Jeep sitting in the grayish light made me itch to find out what that machine was made of. I buckled up and listened to the clean, unadulterated noise, ready to rip as the car awoke.

The Jeep bounced and rumbled as I pulled out of the parking lot, making a beeline to the red mountains and my little bit of freedom. Soon the wind roared in my ears and slapped my face and whispered sweet nothings, causing goosebumps to chase on my skin. Dust clouds tracked me. Sun poured on top of my head, making me long for my cowboy hat left back home. The roughness of the road worked, and the extended suspension caused the seatbelt to press hard against my chest and hip.

When I made it back to the parking lot, I found it mostly empty. I snatched two water bottles, shoved my keys into my jeans pocket, and confidently began my hiking journey on the sandy path with red and white mountains in the distance. This was the best bachelor party a man could ask for.

Sturdy cactus claimed their territory with prickly

spines. The green skin, and its sprouting array of golden yellow flowers, displayed not only hardiness but glory with its greens and yellows, contrasting with the red dirt. I hadn't spotted any animals except blackbirds dancing far above me. I walked more slowly than the young hikers who outpaced me. Clouds gathered into thick clusters. Red dirt crunched under my feet, telling me an ancient story of its own.

I felt alive.

I wished I'd brought Maggie.

At last, after walking steadily up the path, I made it to the top to find a large natural bridge ascending over a deep ravine that descended hundreds of feet.

My shirt clung to me from sweat, and my stomach clenched as I stood on the natural bridge far above everything. It was a long way down. The sun was on its slow descent, retiring from a day's work. The rays spilled onto my face, causing my skin to tingle like it sometimes did when I was with Maggie.

I *really* wished I'd brought Maggie. She had to be as stressed out from this hectic production schedule as I was. But then, she loved this wedding prep stuff, right? She seemed to be in her element.

Except when she put on the dress. And when she got upset about Dee wanting other women's flowers on the cake. And when she wanted to get away for ice cream.

Maybe she wasn't loving this as much as I thought.

As I stared down the mountain, weariness crept up on me, letting me feel my age. I stopped to recover my breath. Animals scurried in the brush. Branches rustled from the breeze, and the sun lowered a few degrees in the sky. I had spent too long on the bridge absorbing everything. I took a sip from my water bottle, wishing that I had brought more water.

Maybe I was seriously out of shape. Maybe the work-outs for the show had been too much or hurrying up the mountain wasn't a good idea. But whatever it was, I was too tired to keep going. I found a large rock to slump against to rest my achy back.

A gentle wind tickled my ears. I closed my eyes and felt the caresses on my skin from the soft wind and soothing rays of the afternoon sunlight. I reached out and touched the pulse of the warm earth tickling my fingertips. My fingers vibrated, absorbing the rhythm of the landscape, the wind, and the sun. I sunk deeper into the ground as the comfort of nature seeped into me. My thoughts settled and breathing slowed. I heard other hikers in the background, but eventually they faded.

A big gust picked up, bringing a chill. I faced the sun, feeling the soft sand under me, and hearing the occasional scurry of a critter. Time passed, and the warmth of the sun was no longer on my face. A chill seeped around me.

"Relax," the wind whispered.

I would relax… if I wasn't about to get married. Which brought up every single thought about Irene, every memory, every broken moment of our marriage. But the breakages weren't sharp edged.

When had façades become enough in that marriage?

An owl hooted. My heart had broken with Irene. All the dreams, plans, all the hope we had cultivated had trans-formed to rot. And I'd let it happen. I'd played the game, kept up the façade, and in the end, lost a lot more than my wife.

Could that happen with Maggie, too?

I thought about her wearing the wedding dress I'd picked out, looking unhappy while she smiled at me.

I thought about how she looked when I declared we could stay home and eat soup instead of going out to a restaurant. Was that all a façade?

A blue glow from the full moon washed onto me, bathing me.

Later, after a long time sitting in the cold evening, a new truth bubbled to my awareness. The heart has many layers. When it breaks, there are more layers. Always. That was a curious thought.

Layers.

That was why I could love Maggie. That was why we could be together. My heart had layers. Had I steeled my heart because I didn't know I had layers?

CHAPTER 15

$\mathcal{M}$aggie

I GLANCED at my phone again. Nothing. Again. Nothing from JT all day. I thought he'd check in at least once. See how I was doing, tell me about his hike, but no. I sighed to relieve the nervous twitters in my stomach. I pushed the pile of wedding samples and papers away.

Completely checking out was probably normal behavior for a guy. He was going into his den or dungeon or whatever John Gray called it. I had thought he would come and kiss me passionately goodbye, but he didn't. No one even saw him grab coffee. He was in a hurry.

Dee soon joined me, and we continued to work into the evening. After I said goodnight to her, I glanced out my hotel window at a soupy blackness. My stomach swirled like a busy washing machine. The roiling stomach happened often when I was young, when my mom was out partying. I eventually developed ulcers.

But JT wasn't partying. I didn't need to worry. "JT isn't my mom. He isn't her," I muttered to myself as I picked up the loose ends in my room. I wanted it clean and tidy if he did visit me after he arrived back. He better come. I put that thought off for another five minutes before I couldn't resist the urge and I texted him to come to my room. I wanted to see he was back and safe. It would help me sleep.

JT had warned me he might be late. He told me to have a night on the town with Dee. I couldn't imagine. *That* I didn't need. I apparently needed to expect JT to be gone for a while. This was how men recharged and fell in love with their women. He needed to be away from me to miss me.

The thought made me feel awful.

Not knowing what else to do, I ordered food delivery, trying not to think of all the trips JT would often take for his work. He didn't build an empire by sitting home, twiddling his thumbs. The food arrived, and smells of spicy chicken casserole penetrated the hotel room. Fantasy notes of New Age music played to calm my nerves, but it wasn't working, and I could barely choke down bites of food. He'd have to take me with him on his trips in the future. That would be better than staying home.

I glanced in the direction of the hotel door then walked over to pull back the thin taupe-colored drape, searching for a sport utility. A car pulled in, its headlights shining on the base of the thin trunk of a cactus. I couldn't make out the driver, who was over five feet away, but he had flipped on the overhead light and left the engine running. I grew tired of watching, and I slumped back to my meal.

My phone rang. "Austin!"

I nestled down on the large sitting chair. My boy rarely called. "Something wrong?" I ventured. "Is it Darlene?"

He sniffed. "She's not coming back. She's still with that guy she took off with at that one party we had at JT's before you moved here." His voice broke.

He needed to let her go. No girl was worth all this pain he put himself through. "It's her loss."

He gasped raggedly, as if life was crumbling around him. "I got down on bended knee in the middle of the airport. But she said no. Why did I keep trying, believing we could work?"

I fiddled with the couch pillow. "I'm sorry you're hurting so badly. I know it's hard."

He shifted. "It is."

"What do you need to get over her, do you think"

We talked about some possibilities until finally, Austin found himself in a good spot. He told me he loved me before getting off the phone. Still no JT. I called and texted with no response. Where was he?

I called Olivia. Before she could say anything, I launched into the situation. "Apparently, JT is MIA. What am I supposed to do?" I spotted a wrinkle on the bedspread and straightened it.

"Give him time." Olivia sounded like an old wise woman bestowing her wisdom patiently on me. "Things will work out."

That advice sounded familiar and very, very empty.

"Men often bolt right before a wedding."

Again, not helpful. After getting off the phone with Olivia, my concern switched from a slight worry to tears. Too many memories of things going sour when there were no-shows in my life. Mom passed out on the street. Mom stuck in some strange alley with our only car's tires slashed. Mom just not coming home. When she did, two days later, no excuse, bags under her eyes with smells of cocktails, of throwing-up, smoke, pot, and sweat.

I sat on the chair, drumming my fingers against the arm, my blood pumping, and my heart racing like running a marathon. I had to do something. I couldn't just sit and wait. I picked up the phone and called the front desk, then the crew to see if they had seen anything.

"Nothing."

I called Austin's phone again, fully aware that when he did look at the phone he'd think I'd lost it.

I explained the situation. "That's unusual," he said with thick sleep in his voice.

Finally, someone who understood my concern. "I'm thinking about calling the cops."

"Don't. JT knows how to take care of himself. Give him another day or two."

"Day or two!" I yelled over the phone. "I can't go a day or two without knowing."

"Mom, he probably left his phone somewhere and isn't around to answer it."

I sniffed. "I could see him doing that. Maybe." That had to be it. Right?

"He probably left it in his car. He's probably sound asleep."

* * *

SEVERAL MINUTES AFTER ONE A.M., I stood outside, looking at the parking lot. This land swallowed up people's souls and left an emptiness in its place. Blackness that spread over the land like a consuming plague.

I stumbled through the spooky hotel grounds to the front entrance and waited for someone to show up at the front desk. A young irresponsible girl ambled to the counter. "Yeah?"

I flashed my license and demanded a key to JT's room.

"You're the lady who keeps calling," the girl accused.

I brushed my hair behind my shoulder.

"Twenty times," she muttered under her breath. "You'd think you'd could have gotten a grip, or someone would take away your license to dial."

"The key, please." I needed to get in JT's room. I needed to see his body spread out on the bed in a deep sleep... forgetting to contact me. He'd crack an eye open, smile, and pull me into his arms where we'd fall asleep entangled together. I just needed to know he was okay.

The teenybopper mumbled something about complimentary breakfast and Wi-Fi, but I closed my eyes and pictured opening the door and seeing JT. Having him pull me tight to his firm chest, rest his chin on my head, and whisper he was fine and sorry. I might be moments away from his comfort if he was in his room.

Armed with a key, I marched into the crisp evening air and to his room. I jabbed the plastic card into the key holder. The door slipped opened into the big dark room.

The drapes were pulled shut. The clock beside the bed glowed with red numbers: 1:01.

Coldness ripped through my body.

My hands patted the wallpaper and flipped on the light switch. I looked across the room to the empty bed. The bedspread had wrinkles. The only other sign of him was a small suitcase by the curtains.

One o'clock in the morning and he wasn't back.

Too scared to investigate on my own in the mountains, the night manager called the cops. Apparently, there had been a murder a few weeks ago in lovely Sedona that had put residents on edge. The police showed up in their pressed blue uniforms with guns. They gave me a rote response that forty-eight hours had to pass before they'd put out a missing person alert. Helpfully, they pointed out that it was more likely he'd gotten caught up at a bar.

I slumped onto JT's bed and tugged a fluffy pillow out from under the covers. I hugged it to me as though it was my life support.

* * *

JT

A bright light pressed on me. I blinked and opened my eyes to see dirt. I lay in a fetal position on the ground with the morning dripping upon me. Pain shot up my spine and down my legs. Cold had sunk deep into me, and my mouth was full of cotton. I gingerly sat up, careful to not make the pain worse. I gathered my empty water bottle.

Birds chirped noisily all around, creating quite a racket.

Red bite marks itched on my arms. I'd pay for this adventure. With effort, I pulled myself to my feet, needing the bathroom at the beginning of this trail, also water. Before leaving my sacred spot, I put my hand on the sand where I had lingered for all those hours. The energy of the Earth swelled up into me. Reinforced, I headed down the mountain bathed in the startling morning light. The rocks had a dust-rose hue. My eyes indulged in its decor of rocks, desert willows, with distant yellow flowers fully expressing its glory.

But enough of desert glory. Maggie must be insane with worry.

Once I was driving, I noticed my blinking phone. I must have finally gotten into cell range.

* * *

Maggie

A noise thumped at the door. I jerked in the sheets. I wasn't asleep, so it didn't wake me exactly, but it drew me out of a foggy state. I stumbled to the door and flung it open to find a disheveled JT struggling with the doorknob.

"JT." I flung my arms around him even though his arms were full of water bottles, keys, pamphlets, and trash. I pressed into all of it, not minding them or his stink. "You're alive." Tears overtook me. My legs weakened, and I shrunk into his arms.

"Maggie?" his voice had a question in it. "What's going on?"

"Where were you?" I couldn't hold back the tears. My eyes had become huge puffballs, and my head ached from sobbing.

Walking forward, bumping me along with him, JT said, "Let's get inside. We'll work everything out."

I grabbed onto his forearm, not daring to let him go, even though he smelled like the concentrated stench of old clothes in a locker room. He was here. He was alive, and he was kind. That was all that mattered.

He dropped everything onto the floor, then flipped on the overhead light to reveal a sun-baked face, arms, and neck. His skin had transformed to a toasty red. Dirt covered him from his hair down to his filthy tennis shoes. Mean red scratch marks ran on his forearms, and bug bites spread from his face and neck, and down his arms. His hair was dulled from grease, though a few strands of gray managed to pop out.

I gasped. "You look awful."

He cast his tired eyes on me. "I bet I don't look as bad as I feel."

I gave a shaky laugh and let go of his arm to wipe my eyes. "I thought something terrible happened. I thought you had died."

He pulled me to him. "I'm sorry."

"Where were you?"

"Hiking."

I rubbed at my eyes to clear sleep and get a good look of him. Definitely sunburned, lots of dirt, and tired. "You okay?"

"Yeah," he muttered, giving me no idea, really, of his condition.

"You don't seem all right. You said you wanted me not to hold things back from you. I ask the same thing."

"Just tired."

"You have a nasty sunburn."

He shrugged.

"I'll see if the crew has any aloe vera."

He stood at the foot of the bed. "Don't worry about that."

I grabbed onto his shirt and twisted it into a big wad in my hand. "You shouldn't have left me like that. You scared me."

His shoulders slumped even more.

"Don't ever do that again. Promise you won't do that again." My voice broke.

He engulfed me into his arms and stroked me. "I'm not going anywhere. We have a simple, quiet life to get back to."

His words tore into me.

Not going anywhere.

Simple, quiet life.

"Hey, babe?"

"Yeah?" I whispered.

"Let's go to snuggle in my bed for a little bit before we have to get up."

JT

The way Maggie held to my arm and kept reaching out and touching me to make sure I was there for the next hour warmed my heart. I liked seeing her soft side. I could still feel her trembling. All I wanted to do was to tuck her into my arms and hold her tight until she stopped shaking. She had worried most of the night. Apparently, she had even called the cops. That was love. I kissed her one more time on the top of her head.

"When I was on the mountain, I sat there under the moon and realized I loved you."

Her eyebrows furrowed. "You didn't before?"

"Of course, I did, but this is different."

"How?" her voice came out soft and tentative.

"Because I realize my heart has layers."

"What does that mean?"

"That my heart is free to love you."

CHAPTER 16

M aggie

AROUND EIGHT IN THE MORNING, I woke to the sound of a bird chirping in the far distance. I found myself nestled in JT's arms. He stunk and still had dirt plastered to him, but I lingered, spooned in his arms. There was something very comforting about being in his arms. He was breathing heavily, not quite snoring, but it caused a periodic jet of air to tickle past my face. Once we were married, every morning could be like this—us waking together.

The day started off slow with the show. We didn't shoot any scenes. Instead we did a lot of outtakes about how we felt about the upcoming wedding. I hardly saw JT, but before we separated for the last evening apart, we kissed long and hard.

That kiss, though, didn't stop me from tossing and turning, even with the lack of sleep the previous night.

Being unable to sleep the night before a wedding was unbearably cliché. Despite that, I lived the cliché because I spent the night wiggling in my bed unable to find a position to lure me into sleep.

In hours, I would be flying in a hot air balloon with JT standing by my side. The violinists would grace the landing strip with in their western cowboy skirts and fashionable white cowboy hats. That was a picture-perfect idea, and all of America would watch. For some reason, though, I wasn't excited.

When my hairdresser knocked on my door to begin prep, I opened the door on the first knock, weariness weighing me down. She was all smiles and full of chatter. Dee had the hotel send up breakfast. I was to eat before slipping into my dress. All I could manage to get down was half a cup of chamomile tea, and one bit of granola. The rest of the food remained un-eaten.

"Time to slip into your dress," my dresser said with a smile.

My hand shook, my stomach swam. I wasn't this nervous the first time I got married. Maybe I should be this anxious. I looked at the white traditional dress, all pressed and hemmed and so-o-o not me, and felt like crying.

* * *

JT

The sound of the alarm dragged me awake from a deep sleep. Apparently, it had been ringing for a long time. Good. That meant I was relaxed for the big day. I'd had been a lot more nervous with Irene. Maybe calmness came with age, or maybe it came with the knowledge that I had picked the right woman. This woman loved me. I had no doubt, and she was fun and willing to blend into my life. I was lucky.

I jumped out of bed. My hips still screamed about the steep incline of the mountain I had climbed two days before. My calves cramped, and my knees threatened to buckle. The perk of endless go-power from my youth had obviously fled.

After climbing into my tux, I headed straight for the supermarket as instructed by Dee. My dreams of food died the moment I pulled into the parking lot in the early morning light. A big red firetruck parked in the middle of the lot. It was the anchor for a hot air balloon.

Fabric spread out along the ground, trailing behind the wicker basket. People and cameras milled everywhere. I looked at the flimsy basket and shook my head. Dots of sweat popped on the back of my neck. People stood in a misshaped semi-circle around the balloon with the sky a cloudless dull grey behind them. Laying out the balloon on the pavement of a grocery store lot seemed like a bad idea. They should pick grass. My hands froze on the steering wheel as more people gathered into the even more lopsided circle.

A knock tapped on my window. I gasped, tearing my eyes away from the crowd to a figure who stood outside my car door. Before I could respond, my door opened to production. "Ready?"

I unbuckled my seatbelt. It snapped back into place. Slowly, I nudged my stiff body out of the car, blood pounding in my head. I didn't like this air balloon thing. I looked over at the production. "You aren't going to make us get in that flimsy basket, are you?"

A sudden scurrying sound of commotion stirred at my side as cameramen zoomed in on us, believing I was about to make a scene. I flipped my head all the way around to the other side of the car to see Dee's chalky face with a set jaw. Today's outfit choice—holey jeans— when was it anything different? Holey T-shirt, too. So, she'd down-graded her normal fashion even more. Greasy hair, nothing unusual. She accessorized with dangling headset wires around her neck, signaling she was about to make things happen. "Can you believe you finally made it to the commitment?"

"Where's Maggie?"

"You look handsome as ever in that suit. That will win America's hearts."

"If I don't die first. With the fabric draped on the ground like this, it'd be so easy for it to snag on a brush or cactus, and create a hole."

Dee plopped her hands on her hips. "These guys know what they're doing."

My stomach twisted. The light on the camera facing me couldn't be ignored. America watched. I closed the door to my car with a snap and waited for the team to fill the balloon. As soon as they were done, I strolled over and mounted the basket like I would a horse. The wind tickled the collar of my shirt.

Maggie hurried in the distance in her long white gown, looking like the most beautiful woman in the world. She made it into the balloon with her dress, tucking its fullness into the corners of the enclosure.

When she came close to me, she wrapped her hands around my arm and cast her baby blues on me. She smelled of morning dawn. Her silky blonde hair fluttered in the wind as she gave me an endearing smile. I pecked her lips, ignoring the rush of the fire shooting up to keep the balloon filled. Maggie tucked her arm around mine and with her other hand strummed her fingers against my arm.

I closed my eyes and focused my attention on the sensation of her touch and the light kiss of the wind. Heat gusted from the fire lifting the balloon, but I forced my thoughts back to Maggie's caresses. They calmed me like a purring cat. I laid one hand on the rim of the basket, and wrapped the other arm around her waist.

"Isn't it beautiful?" Maggie oozed.

To answer her question, I'd have to open my eyes. I pulled them open to see the large looming rugged mountains I had stared at all week. The red monoliths shot into the sky, declaring their permanence. The sun had risen high in the sky and radiated down with hot gusts on the landscape rolling with spots of wildflowers and rocks. I refused to move from where I stood or to look down. Maggie rested her head against my arm.

"Is this a big enough grand entrance for you?"

I closed my eyes again. "Sweetheart, all I need is to be with you."

Maggie

I shivered as I peered at Sedona from the balloon. At first, when we climbed in the basket, my anticipation buzzed, but then we rose in the air, drifting over the same landscape of trees and mountains we had been looking at for days. JT didn't say anything, and the pilot didn't want to interfere with our time. It had, in fact, grown quite dull even though we flew toward our wedding. I was still not feeling well.

When we landed, everything would change. I was literally floating into a new marriage, a new life, a new culture, a new way of being. I was floating into a world so completely different than I had ever known. For this past month, I'd been catching glimpses of this new world full of nature, and I wasn't sure who I was becoming in it. I wasn't even sure if I liked it.

I glanced down at my dress… just like every other wedding dress. I tugged on the loose waist. Apparently, I had lost weight in this new life in a few short days.

I shivered into JT. He pulled me tighter to him. If I said anything, the cameras would pick it up and share it with the world. Neither of us wanted that.

After this balloon ride and the ceremony today, we'd head off to a week in the mountains. Those mountains, I thought, as I looked over the edge of the balloon. A week in that dirt, those trees, and this light wind.

JT had suggested we buy a pop-up bed for camping. I looked over at him. His square jaw drawn tight. He was handsome in the tux. I was lucky, lucky, lucky, to be with him. All the women in America wanted him, and I got him.

Lucky.

I glanced at the balloon pilot. He checked to make sure the fire heated the air in the balloon to the right temperature to keep us aloft. He turned off the fire. We floated in silence. I opened my mouth to ask him about how the whole operation worked, but the silence of the atmosphere seemed foreboding. Or forbidding. So, I closed my mouth again.

I was getting used to swallowing my words.

Lucky.

Movie stars escaped to Sedona. I was on TV. The wedding of my dreams. We had a large cake waiting for us. If it was outside, I bet we would be able to see it from here.

Lucky.

"There's the spot," the pilot said.

The news didn't settle well with my stomach. We would descend, then it would be the ceremony. My palms started to sweat.

As we descended, I heard the pilot curse. "Hold tight, a wind gust brought us down too fast." Before I could grab anything for balance, the far corner of the basket hit the ground, propelling the balloon forward. Both men tumbled onto me, crushing my knee into the basket. I screamed in pain.

JT and the driver scurried quickly off me and made sure the basket sat upright. JT pulled me to my feet as I limped and grimaced. My knee pulsed as I tried to determine if I'd be able to use it. Heat erupted from my entire body.

"I'm so sorry," the pilot said.

Shock pressed in. It felt metaphoric. Me, pinned in one place, not able to move. Not able to speak my mind. Or maybe just not willing to risk what it would cost.

My knee throbbed, my head ached, my dress—the dress I hated and had agreed to wearing in order to keep this man—bore a rip at least four inches long right in front. And, all of this … on my wedding day on national TV.

Tears stung my eyes.

I picked up the dress and pulled it above my knee. Drops of blood stained my skin. Rug burns swelled in red protest.

"You're bleeding," JT said. "Are you okay?"

He bent over to touch me, but I pulled away from him and started crying.

Not happy crying on my wedding day.

Not hurt crying because I had just had two, two-hundred-pound men fall on and injure me.

I wasn't even crying because I hardly slept from panic the last two nights in a row. I cried because this was wrong.

I didn't want to be pinned down. I didn't want to get good at shutting up. I didn't want to have to shut it down, not even for a millionaire cowboy.

"This isn't working." I tossed my dress back down my leg to cover the damage.

"Your knee?" He stood straight. "We need to get a medic."

"No," I said, tugging on his pant leg. "Stop. I am not talking about that. I am talking about our relationship."

JT's face had become unreadable, of course. He mastered his expression during high tension.

"Why do you do that? Whenever we see things differently, you become extremely hard to read."

He remained expressionless. "What are you talking about?"

I shook my head. That was who he was. I was the complete opposite. "I doubt if I have a calm bone in my body." I wiped at the tears, which had become a downpour. "Everyone always knows when I'm upset."

"True."

I snapped my eyes onto him. Him agreeing didn't help. I started making those gross crying noises they would replay on the promos for the show over and over.

"Sweetheart, that's who you are. You don't need to sob about it. It's endearing."

I shook my head. Although he was trying, he didn't understand. He was trying hard. I have to give him credit but, at times like this, I just wish he understood me.

I didn't care if I was a chaotic mess. In fact, I really liked that part of me, and I missed her. I really did. I used to have so much fun, but ever since I hooked up with JT, the fun had vanished. Instead, I became filled with worry about him and making him happy.

Because why? Because I was scared I couldn't make myself happy. I thought I needed someone else to do it for me.

I looked down at my wedding gown with its white flowers dangling by a thread.

"I hate this dress."

"But—"

"And I would rather be beat by a whip than stay in the desert for a whole week."

His shoulders dropped.

"You never said anything."

"You are hard to talk to. It's like we aren't in a real relationship where we are free to talk. Everything is a deal to you."

"That's not fair. If you don't speak up, I think everything is fine."

I wiped at the tears that dripped down my face, my makeup most likely dripping. "I'm speaking now. I don't like animals. I may never like them. I don't hate them. I'm not cruel to them. I don't wish them harm. I just want them to stay in their world, and I'll stay in mine. You can't make them like me, and no amount of exposure is going to lure me over to the animal loving side. You can't sweeten the pot to get compliance."

I stopped talking for a second to catch my breath. "You said crystals and nature were the same. But they're not. They're not to you, and they're not to me. We're different, and that has to be okay. If I said, 'Hey, holding this crystal is as relaxing as a hike, so let's skip the hike and hold crystals.' Would you be okay with that? No. Because that's not *you*. And backcountry camping into deep valleys with bobcats lurking around isn't *me*."

JT's face had transformed to a deep red. "You can't pretend to be okay with something and then get mad at me because I didn't guess that you actually *aren't* okay. That's not fair."

I glared at JT, whose face was still expressionless. I didn't like him saying that. I could feel anger rising. But he was right. There were so many times in the past month I swallowed what I really wanted—from not mentioning my discomfort in his house, pretending I wanted a horse ride at the wedding, not speaking up about my utter dislike about the idea of camping for a week as a honeymoon, among other things.

He had a point. Yet, I wasn't done making mine. "You

want me to come experience nature the way you do, but you won't even close your eyes and give a vortex a chance. You're trying to bring me into your world, but you're not taking a step into mine."

"That is not true. I bought you a hot tub and came up here to Sedona to be in your world. Even went shopping and went to some energy healer."

"That was for TV." My voice quivered. "It wasn't for me. Look, we can make points all day, and in the end, we're pretending. We aren't in a real relationship. I'm scared to death, and you're trying to make a deal. To negotiate us into marriage, yet we can't even have a real conversation. It's like we're—"

"A façade," JT finished in a flat voice. All the flush was gone from his face.

"Yeah," I whispered.

Tears poured, and my throat tightened into a choke hold. "I love you, but I can't do this."

JT sat next to me in the balloon. He seemed to be waiting my emotions out like this upset was a storm that would eventually blow over if he held on long enough.

It wasn't going to pass.

I needed to make that clear.

My emotions were telling me something, and I'd been ignoring than long enough.

"I'm quitting the 'pick me' game."

He looked at me, so confused. At last, his face was readable. He had no idea what I was saying.

"Ever since I got on that damn reality TV show, I have been competing with other girls to gain your attention. Our relationship was formed in that mode, and it is like I have never climbed out of it. I am still being the pathetic, insecure girl trying to win her man." I took a deep breath, taking in all I was saying. "Yuck! I hate that. *That* isn't who I am."

My chest pounded, but at least I had stopped crying.

"I miss me." I sniffed. "I used to be so confident being my quirky self. I used to be fun and laugh and hang out with lots of people. I liked being the party. I want to be her again! I know I got in trouble. I know the nation loved to beat me up over it, but that person I liked. I don't like this person who holds herself back and wears white traditional wedding dresses to please her man. It's not worth it. You are great, JT. I adore you, but it isn't worth not being me."

JT had become extremely white. "Then be her."

That broke something inside me. "I can't be with you and be her." I couldn't look in his eyes. I didn't want to see the hurt in his face. The camera crept closer to capture a close up of the drama. A "rating-boosting" drama. My moment of pain.

I stumbled to my feet using the side of the air balloon basket to hoist me up. I used my right hand to shield my face from the camera as I tried to huff myself over and out. I wasn't going to wait for the stool. I wasn't going to wait for JT to respond to me. I wasn't going to wait for my emotions to calm down and to make me weaker. I was leaving now while I still was clear on what I needed to do.

I needed to escape JT, the man I loved, the kind man who only wanted the best for me, the man who made my heart race like no other man ever had or ever would. I had to go now… to save myself.

The basket was too high for me to elegantly flip out of.

237

Rather, I hefted myself on the basket edge, balancing my ribcage against the wicker. I struggled to lift my leg and dress to the edge. I kept swinging my leg until, at last, my toes caught the rim, and I was able to maneuver my body over the edge with a lot more rug burns and more ripping and snagging of my dress.

Somewhere in the middle of all this, I lost my shoes but, once my feet touched the grass, I ran for maybe ten steps before my dress tangled, and I stumbled. I didn't let it slow me down for long. I had to get away. I had to find myself a new life. One that included me.

"Maggie," I heard people calling after me.

"Let her go." That had to be JT's voice. "No cameras either or I'll sue."

I stumbled along in the trees until I found a secluded patch of grass. I slumped on it, not concerned about grass stains or anything else. This dress was in shambles, anyway... the one bright spot about this whole thing. I picked at the grass and tossed away one blade at a time. The sky changed colors, transforming into oranges and reds.

I remained there, pulling at the grass until the ground was nearly bare. JT had come up and sat a few feet away, not saying a word. I couldn't look up. Instead, tears rolled down my face. They came harder. We remained in that silence for a long time, hearing only the distant noise of our guests, camera crew, and a few songs from the birds in the trees.

I pulled off the chords to my mic. I tossed the base into the trees. I had tried to hit the trunk of a pine tree but missed by a long shot. Like I'd been doing a lot in this relationship. Missing the mark.

"Are you mic'd?"

"No." JT looked at the mic I'd thrown. "This is over?"

Tears pressed against my eyelids. I wiped roughly at them. "Baby," I tried to find my voice. "I love you."

"But—" he choked.

"I have to go." My voice came out rough, edgy, weak, but I charged ahead. "I truly wish you the best, but I have to go. I can't be someone else anymore. I just can't. Not even for *you*. I have to be me, and that has to be enough. I can't fit into your world."

I couldn't look him in the eyes. I peered at the wedding gown—dirty, torn, and still ugly. "I am a red gown sort of girl, not off-white. And you need the off-white girl."

* * *

JT

I stared at Maggie's hair tossed in every which way, eyes swollen pink, face flushed with red. My throat constricted around all the words I wanted to say. All the deals I wanted to make. My whole life had been a deal.

From the moment my dad told me life was about what a person negotiates, I'd felt driven to negotiate well. I'd been working it. Making money. Building a corporation. Being a huge success. Playing a role.

And now, the only way I knew how to handle things being ripped away by the most important person in my life, was to make a deal. She wasn't having any of it anymore and I had no idea what to say that wouldn't sound like a deal.

"I don't care about your dress," I managed to say.

"Ha!" Maggie said with a lot of anger. "You care about everything. Or, you care how it *looks*. I can't become you, nor do I want to."

I blinked hard. What was she talking about?

She tossed a piece of grass with gusto. "I am not going to like the wild—I don't like wild animals lumbering around everywhere. I don't like 118-degree summers. I need grass—the real stuff with dirt, not that plastic turf that emits chemicals. I need to wear high heels and clothes that sparkle. I need to have room to be myself, leave shoes on the floor and not have every soup can in lines a quarter of an inch apart from one another. Plus, I can't stay in a town indefinitely. I need night life." She had stopped talking for a moment gasping for air.

"You make staying with me sound like a jail sentence." My eyes narrowed. "If you really are this miserable, maybe you would be better off on your own?"

She looked at me with a tight jaw.

"Maybe you should take a break, Maggie. Visit the city, see some of your old friends, and later we can—"

Her eyes flashed at me, old, fiery Maggie. "Stop. Making. Deals. Can't you hear what I'm saying? I don't fit in your world. There's no space for me."

A fist tightened around my heart. "No. I think you're saying, if I love you, I should let you go."

She lowered her gaze, avoiding my eyes and nodded. "If that's the deal you want to make, yes, you should."

CHAPTER 17

T

T HE HOUSE LOOMED dark and empty when I arrived home
early in the morning. I had to stay late at the wedding ceremony to deal with the media.

Dee hadn't exploded like I expected when she learned
the wedding was off. Instead, she went very pale, and said
almost nothing, just shoved my belongings in the car and
slammed my door as a way to say goodbye.

I had no idea where Maggie was or what she planned to
do. I had offered her a place in my guesthouse until she
landed on her feet, but she flat-out refused. I flipped on
lights and stumbled my way to the refrigerator. Inside sat a
small portion of a casserole Maggie had baked before we
left to Sedona. Chances of it still being any good weren't
strong.

I picked it up and pitched the whole thing into the trash. The glass shattered. I never wanted to see that darn, perfect casserole dish again. I opened the freezer to find a frostbitten pizza. I chucked that in the pail, too.

Time for soup. In a can. Right from my cupboard. My way. I didn't have to adapt anymore, right? I opened my cupboard to find three tomato soup cans left. They were a quarter inch apart. I stared at them. All three faced me with perfect attention. Placing the cans in perfect order was kind of ridiculous. I moved one can over an inch, which shook up the perfect alignment.

Feeling the freedom of that act, I dared to turn two of the cans in different directions.

The third can I warmed up, then flung myself onto the couch and flipped on the TV. Time to disengage. Time to forget the debacle that was my life… The screen blared, and I stared at an image of our wedding with a subtitle in a big red font: *"Wedding Cancelled Hours Before Ceremony."* It cut to footage of me looking completely shell shocked—well, they got that part right—and Maggie sitting on the grass, hands over her face.

That image sliced into my heart. I went to the guest house, opened its sliding glass door, and stepped in. Silence. No one was there. All that remained was her lingering scent and her touches on the décor. Unable to handle smelling her, I stomped back into the house and opened the cup cupboard. My cups weren't in straight lines or exactly inches apart any more. Maggie's doing.

Maggie loved me. I knew she did. I never had any doubt of her love or her sincerity, and I loved her despite letting her slip away, along with all her intensity, passion, love, and headache. Afraid to show how I felt. Afraid to be vulnerable. Afraid to learn what she wanted and needed.

In business, I knew what to do, but with Maggie, I did not. Her words, "I can't be myself while being around you," haunted me. I stared at my bare bedroom walls that Maggie wanted to fill with our happy smiling wedding pictures. I had said no.

I didn't want my room to change. In fact, I didn't want my life to change. I had been plugging her into the Irene spot as... support staff. Maggie would never be contained like that. She was too alive and spontaneous.

And she wasn't having any part of my pretty-making deals. She was right. I spent my life making deals. I made deals instead of having relationships. My whole life had been a deal. From the moment my father taught me the art. Making deals. Making money. Building a corporation. Being a huge success.

I had a choice. Keep on being like the Kinkade painting, like my first marriage—a beautiful lie—or cope with all the messiness of real relationships and get Maggie back.

I knew exactly which I needed to choose. I wasn't going to let this be the final deal with Maggie. At the least, I was going to offer her something else. I was going to *be* something else. For both of us. If she'd have me. I leapt up from the chair and marched to the phone.

I called her. It went straight to voicemail. I called Olivia, who hadn't heard from her either. The stress in her voice told me she was telling the truth. I called Austin. He picked up on the second ring.

"Where is she?" There was a worry in his tone and maybe a bit of blame, too.

"I have no idea."

The conversation didn't go on much longer than that. Neither of us knew anything, but Dee would know. If I found Dee, she would lead me to Maggie. Ten minutes later I was in the car heading for the airport. I called Dee.

She answered on the first ring. "She's safe. Don't worry." She spoke in a rush and with a bit of irritation, but had been expecting my call.

"Is she with you?"

Dee breathed heavy on the phone. She might be outside. It might be the wind making that noise. That was a clue.

"JT, you know I wanted you two to work. I really did, and I mean that more than for the job I am getting fired from."

I rubbed my forehead. This was too much. "Tell me where Maggie is, and I will hire you."

"No can do."

"Dee, I need to know where she is."

"JT, she left you on national TV." Dee hung up.

The only sound in the car was my hammering heart.

Maggie was okay. Dee was watching out for her. That should be enough.

It wasn't.

I had to apologize. I had to let Maggie see I wasn't the man I'd been. That I could change. That I would change. I wiped my palms on my pant leg. Was I being a businessman right now, demanding we come to better terms? Probably. Damn it. It was who I was.

We both had to be who we were. She wasn't the only one who got to be true to herself. I was a damn fine businessman. But that wasn't all I was. It wasn't all I could be. And I'd fight like hell to become something more... for Maggie.

* * *

Maggie

I sat on the grass after the production crew and cameras had left. It was just me and the grass and the wind and this stupid gown.

And Dee. I had no idea why the conniving Dee stuck around when I no longer served a purpose, but she did. She sat on the grass beside me, not saying a word, just sat there, occasionally handing me new pieces of grass to mangle.

"So..." she finally said. "What do you think?"

I gave a grasp. "I think everything's gone to hell."

She nodded. "It sort of has."

"Sort of?"

She shrugged. "You did lose the love of your life—or rather, kicked him to the curb—but you did it for the right reasons."

I looked up. "I did?"

She met my eye. "If you meant what you said, you did."

I looked back at the clumps of mangled grass all around me. "Oh, I did," I murmured. "And I feel awful."

"Well," she hopped to her feet, "There's only one thing to do."

I looked up. The sunset was deepening behind her. I felt like crying. "What?"

"Get you back to the city."

She tugged me to my feet. Maybe that would help. There was nothing for me here anymore. Maybe not anywhere. But at least it would be the real me who had nothing. I felt my heart breaking as I let her lead me away.

* * *

BACK IN THE CITY, a day later, I wasn't much better. I hadn't yet "landed on my feet." In fact, I looked like a train wreck. I felt like one, too. I kept taking deep breaths as I tried to get back into the swing of having a life. I started by checking emails, and there were a lot. All sorts of people wanting interviews and offering condolences and berating me. Again. I closed my eyes and reached out to snap my laptop shut. Not now.

I tried to eat, but only managed to shove in a few crumbs. Everything reminded me of JT—the emails from a ton of curious people, the tea I drank, the horse paintings in the hallway of the hotel, the answers Dee gave to countless calls.

"Runaway bride syndrome," she said over and over, not giving anyone, even her producers, more information than that.

Who would have thought Dee would be the stand-up guy in all this?

By eleven o'clock, she'd been fired and was cussing at the politics of network TV. "You'll land on your feet..." I said, giving her words of encouragement back to her, fully earnest, but only half-hearted, because that's all I had left. Half a heart. The other JT held.

She waved me off.

Three minutes later, she took a phone call out on the porch, darting me quick glances as she talked just outside of earshot.

She hung up the phone and came inside and continued looking at me.

"Uh-oh. Something I should worry about?"

"No." She flopped down onto her chair in front of her side of the desk. "Today's going to be a long one."

I inhaled slowly. "I'm really sorry. I didn't mean to get you fired."

"The job was awful, and I didn't like who I became. I hurt people's lives. Not going to do that anymore."

I smiled a little. "I never thought you'd be the person to come through for me."

She winced. "I have a lot of amends to make."

I sat up straight. Her being fired was my fault. I owned the blame on that. And she was a good producer even if at times I didn't like what she did. "I'll do anything I can to help you. I can give testimonials—not sure how much the woman who ran away from the altar would help, but if you need them, I'm yours. I'll go on TV and say how unfair it is. Anything."

She tapped her pen against the desk. "Can I get back to you on that? You do owe me, and I will collect. But don't talk to any media yet. No one. We need to strategize our next move."

"Move?" I asked faintly.

"You wanted to own your power, and I'm here to see that you do. It'll be good for both of us."

I squinted at her. "What are you talking about?"

247

"Podcast." She waved her hand in the air between us. "Together. You and me. On relationships and why they're so messed up."

Podcast? Yesterday I had planned to be married to the love of my life, and today Dee wanted me to go into business with her. I felt an undercurrent of nerves. My phone buzzed. I jumped and looked at it. My son, calling for a thousandth time.

"I'm okay," I answered it.

"Mom!" His voice choked. He sounded full of panic.

"Baby, it's okay. I am okay."

"What happened?"

I sighed. "Austin, you know how you loved Darlene so much, but you two weren't meant to be?"

"I don't—"

"That's the way it is with JT and me. I love him. He is a good man, but I can't be myself with him. I wore that horrible dress yesterday to be the traditional wife he wanted. But I'm not traditional. I can't be what I am not."

"Mom, you were a stay-at-home mom for almost all my life."

I took a deep breath. "True, but I don't want to do it anymore. I need to be married in a red wedding dress."

He was quiet for a second. "I'm sure if JT knew that meant so much to you, you could wear whatever color you wanted."

"You don't get it. It's his whole lifestyle. It is not me. I love JT the way he is, but there are sometimes when I feel like I am not getting the real him, the real person. I am getting the business JT. I won't live like that anymore. You were right when you once called me a free bird. I guess that is really what I am."

* * *

JT

I sat at the airport waiting for my plane when Dimitri called. I gave him a brief summary of yesterday, ending with, "She told me I treated the relationship like a deal."

"Relationships aren't deals," Dimitri flipped into lecture mode. "Well, at least not romantic ones. Healthy ones. If you leverage by doing "this for that" it feels off. You have to understand what the other person needs and help them get it." Dimitri stopped talking to let that settle. "So, what does she need, and how can you help her get it?"

His words rang in my ears, echoing like a call in a mountain throughout the plane ride. The aircraft landed in the thick afternoon smog. Doubts riddled my mind as I made my way to Dee's apartment door. The address wasn't hard to get after a few well-calculated phone calls placed to the show. I shifted my package to one arm, knocked, then stepped back to see if anyone answered.

Dee did. She said nothing but opened up the door to show Maggie sitting in front of a mirror combing her hair. She wasn't paying attention to Dee or who was at her door.

I strolled over to Maggie and stood inches away. When she peered up at me, she burst into a huge overwhelming ocean of sobs. I hooked my arm around her neck and pulled her close, still holding the package tight with my arm. This caused her ruckus of tears to erupt into even greater waves.

"It's okay," my voice came out deep, strong, like I was on a mission, which I was. I was going to save both our hearts if she would have me.

"JT?" She had questions lining her face. "What are you doing here?"

"I'm here to make you happy. If I can."

She crossed her arms over her chest. "What?"

"I've made a mistake."

The muscles around her jaw tightened. "Go on."

Taking a deep breath, I continued, "I haven't been putting you first. I haven't paid enough attention to your needs. Your wants. I've been thinking about how you fit into the 'deal' I'd already made with life. But I'm done. Done making deals, at least with you. I just want you to be happy, and I truly think I can do it. If… you'll have me."

She blinked. I took that as a good sign she was still listening. "I want you to be happy in this relationship."

I stared at the love of my life, whom I'd chosen to be my wife, but lost. "I have been a fool. I was focusing too much on having you blend in my world, and I didn't take any steps to step into yours."

"No, you didn't." She avoided my eye contact.

"I was pushing too much for my way."

She nodded.

"I don't want to do that anymore."

She glanced at me. "I love you, but I can't be changing me."

"Neither of us are going to change who we are, or what matters most about us. At least, that's not what I want." I hesitated then extended the package. "Here."

She took a step back. "What is that?"

I set the box on her desk and pulled out a heavy red-quartz crystal more than a foot long.

"This is the rarest quartz from Brazil, and to me it symbolizes you. You are rare, beautiful, and quirky as hell. You can have this no matter what, but if you let me back in your life, I think we could make a magical future."

"JT that's so kind, and a wonderful gesture but—"

"I know you can't live in Tucson all the time, but could you live in it part of the time and LA the rest?"

Her eyebrows narrowed. "Are you making a deal?"

I smiled. "Like I said, Maggie, we both get to be who we are. And I can't help it: I make deals. But I promise I'll never, ever try to 'deal' our relationship again. I'll never try to get you to be someone you're not, just because it makes me feel more comfortable."

She tipped her head to the side. "What was that you were saying, about part-time in Tucson?"

My heart sped up. "I have a real estate agent to help us pick out our condo *together*. You get to fill it with energy rocks and sparkle, and whatever else makes you happy."

"You don't like sparkly rocks."

"I actually don't care about sparkly rocks. They just seemed so... unconventional. But you're unconventional. I'm going to stop caring how things *look*. I care what they are. And you're good. *We're* good."

She crossed her arms. "How would that work with your work?"

"Talked to Dimitri this morning. I'm retiring and taking a consulting or work-for-hire position as they need me, but I'll focus most of my time building a life with you. I want us at the center."

"But you love—"

"I love you more."

She paled. "You don't need to do that. A lot of this is my fault. I didn't speak up more. I didn't put us at the center either. I put *you* in there, but not me. That doesn't work."

"Are you ready to do that now?" Our eyes met. "I am."

"Now that I am doing a podcast with Dee on women empowerment, I think I'll have to."

I hesitated. "What?"

"Dee and I decided to work together. We're going to run a podcast on being true to yourself even while you're in a relationship."

Wow. Didn't see that coming. Dee and her tricks. I bit back my protest. If I said I was going to let her live her life, I'd have to actually do it.

"If that's what's right for you." I said, testing the words as they came out.

They felt good.

Maggie raised an eyebrow. "But you don't trust Dee."

"No, but I trust you. If you trust her, then I support you. I'm new at this. I am not sure how to do this, but... is that right?"

She laughed. My heart lifted. "It's pretty good, cowboy." Then she looked serious again. "How can we make this work with me being me, and you being you? We'd have to share our feelings more."

I nodded. "That isn't going to be easy, but I'll do it."

"Why? Because it's part of the deal?"

I thought a moment, then said slowly, "No. Because it's the right thing to do. Because if you get to be you, I get to be me. And I'm going horseback riding sometimes."

"You want me to go with you?"

"If you want."

A smile lifted on her lips. "You'd go out to eat with me?"

I smiled back. "Now who's bargaining?"

The smile lifted her cheekbones. "I learned from the best."

"Yes, baby," I said, "We'll go out to eat sometimes."

"Often?"

"That might be pushing it. I mean, I could imagine a nice dinner out after a long trail ride…"

She broke out in laughter, and I felt, finally, like I could inhale a deep breath.

"You accept that I'm quirky and might make a mess out of everything?"

I laughed. "One of your charms."

She blushed. "Honeymoon in Italy in a villa?"

"Sounds like a great idea."

She squinted her eyes, examining me closely. "I might not always agree with you."

"Perfect." I wrapped my arms around her. "I don't want you to. Where would the challenge be?"

She leaned into my touch. "We might fight more than you did with your first wife."

"As long as I have you by my side, that is what I want."

She tipped her chin back, inviting me to kiss her, which I immediately took her up on. When we stopped kissing, I whispered, "You drive a hard bargain."

"One more thing," she said, eyes intent. "I'm getting married in a red gown, and no dead animal remains anywhere in any house. I just can't deal with that."

"We're a team, Maggie. You're good for me. You make me more of a person."

She shrugged with a smirk on her face. "I guess that's true." She looked up with those big eyes of hers encapsulating me with so much love.

"Turns out, I need you happy more than anything else. Let's call the justice of the peace and get married today."

$\mathcal{M}$ aggie

JT and I filmed the TV wedding after all. I wanted Dee to get her old job back, which took some time to sort out, and we didn't want to disappoint our fans. The TV wedding wasn't everything I had imagined. It was actually a lot of work. Turns out that alongside a man who loved me, I didn't really like having the cameras constantly on me.

But America watching didn't stop me from talking to Austin. On the way into the dressing room where I would be putting on my red silk wedding gown that felt completely like me, I spotted my son down the hall. I grabbed his arm.

"Sorry you haven't found your right person yet."

Austin pulled me in for a tight hug. "I'm happy where I am."

I looked at him and saw how he looked at me. I believed, for now, he would be okay. I hurriedly dressed, glad that Olivia was there with me to steady my nerves. While getting my hair done, I overheard Anna give her opinion to the media about her Grandpa JT marrying the second runner-up. "Maggie isn't as nice as the lady before her."

I stood from my makeup chair and headed around the corner where they filmed. "What do you mean not as nice as Milly."

Anna shrugged. "She was nice."

I forced a smile. "Now, Anna, you know that we're friends. We go to movies and feed the horse and do crafts."

She had a serious expression. "True. Okay…" She thought about it and ran over to me and hugged me tightly.

People around us "ooh'd" and "aah'd."

Dee rushed in as I finished doing my hair. "I'm so glad you're doing this on TV."

I didn't say anything, not sure about it, but willing to help her out.

Dee turned to leave and ran straight into Dimitri. Instead of shoving him out of the way and snapping at him, she reached out and took his hand with a smile.

Dee and Dimitri?! How did that—

"Places everyone," the set manager called.

Time for me to get married on live TV.

JT waited to kiss me until the pastor said, "I now pronounce you…" And JT pounced a kiss on me that filled me up with tingles until Dee ploughed toward us with a funny expression.

"The network wants you both to be in the next *Million-*

aire Engagement show, but this time as the hosts… and have Anna as the commentator. It would be a family thing, and you would have lots of time off. No cameras following you. Plus," Dee waved her eyebrows at me, "It would be great for our *Authentic Love* podcast."

Thank you for joining me on the *Millionaire Romance* journey. If you enjoyed the novel, I would very much appreciate you posting a review on Amazon.

https://amzn.to/2MKcqy6

Sign Up…

Romantic Rants Newsletter

and receive an ebook *Husband Shopping,* which explores what we can learn from reality TV on how to attract a man.

https://www.authoranastasiaalexander.com/

Anastasia Alexander doesn't have the answers to life's love questions. What she does know is that love in the 21st century is complex. There are no easy answers, and there is a lot of richness and juiciness in exploring all the complexity that love brings.

Her credentials are two failed marriages and a current successful marriage (fingers crossed), equaling thirty-one years of marriage and a willingness to believe that the benefits of flirting aren't dead. Since she loves her current husband too much to flirt outside of marriage, she pours her love for flirting into stories.

www.ingramcontent.com/pod-product-compliance
Lightning Source LLC
Chambersburg PA
CBHW061604170626
46811CB00001B/317